What readers are saying about The Batch Magna Chronicles

'An **absolutely delightful, delicious, witty novel**... Priceless characterization, right down to the lovable dogs, and descriptions of flora and fauna by someone deeply in love with the English countryside. It is a stunningly charming tale, one that becomes a part of your heart.'
Henrietta Bellows, Amazon

'I absolutely loved this wonderful book and its colourful characters!... Kudos for **a fantastic reading experience**. I just knew I was going to love it from the very first page!'
Jeri S. Connor, Amazon

'I loved this book! It's lyrical and very amusing, with **all the charm of an old Ealing comedy**... '
Carole Kelcher, Amazon

'You know you love a book when you're a week past finishing it and you're still savouring the language... **I found myself often chuckling, sometimes wiping a tear, and on a few occasions, reading sections aloud to my cat**... '
S. Kay Murphy, On Simply Being True

'I first got this book out of the local library, and then bought a copy – I wanted to read it again and again. It's **a treasure, a smashing read, funny and beautifully written**.'
Anne James, Amazon

'... a lovely romp through a beautifully described English (when it is not Welsh) countryside full of hedgerows, meadows, and misty riverbanks, home to skylarks, peacocks, and an assortment of beloved mutts. The descriptions are to be savoured, not skimmed.
to Batch Magna, and am loc
book in
*Pamela Grandstaff, auth(
Virg(*

G000255845

The GHOST of ARTEMUS STRANGE

THE BATCH MAGNA CHRONICLES, VOLUME FIVE

PETER MAUGHAN

Farrago

This edition published in 2019 by Farrago,
an imprint of Prelude Books Ltd
13 Carrington Road, Richmond, TW10 5AA, United Kingdom

www.farragobooks.com

ISBN: 978-1-78842-135-5

Have you read them all?

Treat yourself to the whole Batch Magna Chronicles series:

The Cuckoos of Batch Magna
Welcome to Batch Magna, a place where anything might happen. And often does...

Sir Humphrey of Batch Hall
The course of true love never did run smooth – especially not when badger baiters are involved.

The Batch Magna Caper
Sparks fly as a real gun and a real crook find their way into a historical re-enactment at Batch Hall.

Clouds in a Summer Sky
The steam boat *Batch Castle* starts carrying passengers once more, leaving local taxi magnate Sidney Acton with a score to settle.

The Ghost of Artemus Strange
Sir Humphrey's plans to play Father Christmas are thrown into doubt, and ghostly goings-on turn more chaotic than planned.

Turn to the end of this book for more information about Peter Maughan, plus – on the last page – **bonus access to a short story** by the author.

To the memory of my mother and father

Chapter One

The bells of St Swithin's, carrying on their ancient sides saints and merchants, squires and parsons, rhymes and prayers, rang out under a moon pale like ice, out over the Marcher village of Batch Magna and its river, where the lamps of the boats were lit and a mist smelt of frost and fires.

The full peal of eight, sweetened by Norman stone, falling in an avalanche of sound, tumbling across fields iron with winter, until lost among the stripped wooded hills of the valley.

The present squire of this March, Sir Humphrey Franklin T. Strange of Batch Hall, the ninth baronet of his line, in a Yankees baseball cap and a shirt with parrots on it, was putting his heart and his considerable weight into it, the rope with its woollen sally coloured like seaside rock leaping in his meaty grip, the giant shadows of the ringers under a naked overhead light moving on the limewashed stone of the tower like ogres, like ancient imaginings.

Humphrey was on the other end of the tenor bell, the heaviest and loudest of them, giving voice with it as if it were something he'd been *bursting* to say but hadn't the words for. The tower captain, a retired headmistress and committee member of the WI, led the dance with the lightest bell, the treble, calling out the ringing changes in tones made for corridors and playgrounds, handstroke and backstroke, bell on bell, their iron tongues speaking over and over, the language of faith and mathematics.

When the bells were silent again and their ropes tied, the narrow spiral stairway of the tower echoed with the ringers' shared pleasure and a job well done. The stone of the stairs sculpted by the centuries, the passage of fellow ringers who had felt the same, and who had made the same journey afterwards to the village pub, within singing distance of its church.

The red dragon of Wales above the entrance of the village post office and shop was a riposte, in this place where England turns into Wales, and Wales back into England round the next bend, to the flag of St George flown from the Steamer Inn. On the inn's sign a paddle steamer was busy making smoke, from a time when the houseboats on the river were working craft, plying the waters of the Cluny and the Severn.

The bell ringers used the bigger of the pub's two bars, a room of worn Welsh slate flagstones and high-backed settles under beams of estate oak, the ceiling varnished a yellow-orange with the smoke of the years, the air scented with logs burning in a fireplace big enough to stable a pony.

Bill Sikes, a large white boxer, with the face of the spike-collared dog in a cartoon backyard, dozed in front of its warmth, sharing it with the pub's two dogs. Bill's owner, Phineas Cook, off the houseboat the *Cluny Belle*, was perched on a bar stool when Humphrey arrived with the others.

'Ah, Humph. Now you've finished drowning out sin, or at least deafening it, with your well-tuned cymbals, have a pint.'

'No, thanks, Phin. I'm just stopping for a quick half with the team here, and then getting back. Hey! I didn't tell ya – we've found a Santa Claus outfit.'

'Ah, good. Where did you—?'

'I didn't. Clem did. After phoning round half the day she found this costumier's in Trehenydd,' he said, his Bronx accent getting to grips with the Welsh language. 'I've got to have a fitting tomorrow. You know?' He patted his ample front and looked doubtfully at Phineas.

'You're just the right size, Humph,' he assured him, 'for the bringing of good cheer.'

'Yeah, well, anyway, they donated it for free when she told them what it was for. How about that?'

'She can be very persuasive, that Clem of yours.'

'You're telling me.'

'I'm looking forward to it. Father Christmas arriving on a paddle steamer.'

Humphrey embraced the thought with a slow, wide grin. 'Yeah. Yeah,' he said, glancing over at Priny Cunningham. It was Commander Cunningham, Priny's husband, who, as skipper of the estate's working paddle steamer, the PS *Batch Castle*, would be bringing Christmas to Batch Magna.

Priny was sitting at the table with Bryony Owen, eldest daughter of Annie Owen, who helped out at the Hall, discussing, at this busy time of the year, business tactics.

Priny, puffing away at a long-stemmed amber cigarette holder, and scented with Guerlain, was dressed for winter in a pink duffel coat and a Cossack-style fur hat, boots and the pearls she was never without, unless it was one of the times they'd gone across a pawnshop counter, to provide marching money, as she and the Commander put it.

Bryony was dressed as if she had a tractor parked outside, which, running a smallholding in the valley, she often did have. She was also the woman who, some time back, had introduced the village to life on the never-never, in the enticements of the home furnishing and clothes pages of mail order catalogues. She had recently gone into partnership with Priny and they were now planning expansion both sides of the border, Priny with the cost of Plymouth gin in mind, and Bryony, a single mother, with Christmas morning and presents under the tree.

Humphrey joined the other ringers with his drink, sitting with them at one of the bigger tables, a tribe apart. The language of the bells, of Kent trebles and the Queen's change, holt's singles, royals and weasels, and grandsire triples, a shared secret. The key to that other world they were taken to, taken to as if hypnotised, or drugged, standing in a circle under the bells as if in obeisance.

A world reached not down a rabbit hole but found up in the air, where arithmetic becomes mystery, a conversation with God.

And the eager clamour of a peal running seemingly pell-mell through its endless changes had for them its own logic, its own perfect sense, as in that of a dream.

Another world to where Humphrey, for one, could briefly

'A friend of Mr Perkins is getting married today,' she told Miss Wyndham. 'In Gerfyn-y-Coed.'

'Oh, how nice!' Miss Wyndham said. 'Church or chapel?'

'Chapel. He's Welsh.' He grinned. 'But what's this about a bloke sleeping in your shed? You full up already, Mrs Owen?'

Annie laughed. 'No, nothing like that, unfortunately. I don't know who he is.'

'A local drunk, maybe?'

'I've no idea,' Annie said.

'Could be, Dad,' Howard said. 'Or he could be dead,' he added, as if not ruling it out, eyes narrowed with the authority of one who had actually seen him.

Mr Perkins looked at the weapons the two women were carrying. 'I'd better come with you.'

'Oh, I couldn't—'

Mr Perkins held up a firm hand. 'It's not a problem, Mrs Owen. I'll just let the missus know first. Elsie!' he bawled up the stairs.

'Dad likes chucking people out,' Howard told the two women. 'We used to have a pub.'

'What shed's he talking about?' Mr Perkins asked.

'Dunno,' Annie said. 'There's lots of them. Didn't have horses in it, did it?'

'No,' Howard said, 'he wasn't in one of them. I saw them sheds. I didn't go in, not with horses in them. Not me. I saw a film once where this man—'

'Elsie!' Mr Perkins shouted up the stairs again.

His wife's head appeared over the banisters from the landing, her hair in large coloured curlers.

'What is it? I'm trying to get ready. And Howard, I want you up here!'

'Got a little problem, love. We'll be back in a jiffy.'

'Yeah, well, just make sure you are,' was all Elsie said, a woman used to life and its little problems.

'Right, you'd better show us then, son,' Mr Perkins said.

They followed Howard round to the side of the house and under the stable yard arch, with its half-timbered gable and cockerel weathervane, and the clock that had stopped at five minutes past some noon or midnight in some long-forgotten year.

He led them straight down the cobbled yard to the coach house beyond the stables.

One of its two large doors was ajar. Mr Perkins pushed it further open and they followed him in.

'He's in there,' Howard whispered, pointing to a large car left over from another age, its power long silenced under dust and cobwebs, sunk in elegant decline on flattened threadbare tyres.

'Blimey!' Mr Perkins said. 'Where's the blooming 'orse?'

'That's Bess, the late General Strange's Bentley Saloon,' Miss Wyndham had him know, defensive of an old memory. 'Named after a favourite hunter of his. There was a keeper in the lodge in those days to man the gates,' she said, sharing that with Howard.

'Get away!' Howard said, having no idea what she was on about but feeling something was called for.

'And a uniformed chauffeur with the family crest as a cap badge. And a speaking tube in the back to—'

'Rupert...' Annie said wonderingly.

She was peering in through the rear open window of the Bentley. 'Hattie – it's Rupert!'

She opened the car door and a chicken hopped out.

'Stone me,' Mr Perkins said, peering over at Rupert sprawled on the back seat of the Bentley like someone who had grown old with it, forgotten like the car itself by time.

Rupert was a gentleman of the road, a professional tramp, a country cousin to the town tramp, in two raincoats greasy with travel and tied at the waist with baler twine, his face ripened and polished with weather like a crab apple, and with a beard among the grime of unsullied downy whiteness, as if he cleaned it regularly, like a cat. All he owned he had with him, an ash stick cut from a hedge, a billycan blackened with the smoke of countless roadside brew-ups.

His other belongings were in two plastic shopping bags sealed in another two bags inside those, suggesting the privacy of a home, the rooms in a life he carried with him over a shoulder with straps of twine looped through the handles.

'Rupert!' Annie said, her voice sharp with concern.

Rupert stirred and looked at her. Whatever had moved him all those years ago to walk away and to keep on walking, still kept its distance in amused-looking eyes of a quite startling clear, bright blue.

'Hello, Annie,' he said.

'We wondered where you'd got to, lovey, back awhile,' she said on a softer note. 'We came out here enough times to have a look, I can tell you.'

'Ventured a bit further north this year, Annie. Never again. Open hands and doors but too hard a road. Hello,

Harriet. I'd doff my hat to you ladies but there's an egg in it. Your chicken woke me letting me know she'd laid it and then kept me company when I dropped off again. But you came prepared for it, I see,' he said, getting out of the car and nodding at Miss Wyndham's frying pan.

'Cor!' Howard said, after getting a proper look at him.

Rupert smiled at him, and glanced guardedly at his father, tramps and small boys being nearer to each other's worlds. 'Good morning,' he said.

Mr Perkins, looking unsure, before deciding on a polite smile, returned the greeting, and then turned to Annie. 'Well, it looks like I can get back then, Mrs Owen.'

'Oh, yes, of course, Mr Perkins. And thank you now. It was good of you.'

'Any time. Come on, Howard.'

'Enjoy the wedding,' Miss Wyndham called after them.

'And you, Rupert,' Annie told him. 'Indoors with you as well.'

'Oh, yes. I should think so!' Miss Wyndham said.

'No need for that. But I wouldn't mind—'

'No, you don't,' Annie said. 'You're coming in. It's freezing in here.'

The three of them followed Mr Perkins and Howard back down the yard to the Hall, Rupert grumbling about being a hostage to winter. And whether that meant one of the spikes he usually tucked himself away in until the earth warmed up again, or here, in the kind but firm custody of the two women, it would start, he knew, in a bathtub.

The room in Batch Hall that, in palmier days, had been the servants' hall, next to the larder that had once been the butler's pantry, was now signposted, in the hall and on its door, as the 'Lounge and Bar, for the use of paying guests'.

But as presently there were no paying guests the family had lit the fire in there and were taking advantage of the facilities, which included a twenty-six-inch colour television set, instead of the twelve-inch black and white they normally watched in the library. Hawis, their young daughter, was noisily chasing one of the dogs, a lurcher, round the room, followed by a yapping Jack Russell, until told again to sit down by Shelly, Humphrey's mother, who was holding the baby, Ralph Franklin T. Strange II, while watching the television.

Rupert and the baby's father were playing draughts and drinking Sheepsnout cider, a brew that had in its golden strength the heat of a summer that seemed even more distant now, with its ice-cream weather and the bounty of outdoor revenues, such as full decks for the summer delights of day trips on the PS *Batch Castle*, the paddle steamer that had once plied a Victorian Thames.

It was a younger-looking Rupert, a Rupert more of this world, sitting at the table with Humphrey. Scrubbed up and trimmed, and wearing a new set of second-hand clothes which Clem had got from the Shrewsbury Salvation Army, including a British Warm overcoat against winter and a sturdy pair of brogues to replace the black patent leather pumps he'd salvaged from a dustbin, and taken on a last, slow dance from the hard roads of the north to the edge of Wales.

'See, Rupe, this game's called checkers in the States,' Humphrey said, jabbing with a meaty finger at the board between them, as if to suggest the reason Rupert was winning so heavily.

'Well, we'll call it checkers, Humph, if you think it will help,' Rupert offered mildly, and took another two of his pieces. 'I haven't played for forty years, maybe longer. Like riding a bike, I suppose. One never forgets.'

'Yeah,' Humphrey muttered.

'You'll never guess, Clem,' Shelly said, dragging her eyes away from the television when Clem returned from answering the phone in the hall. 'It's the king. The distinguished mystery guest coming to dinner at Eaton Place,' she went on, when Clem looked blank. 'King Edward the Seventh. Defender of the faith and Emperor of India and the dominions beyond the seas, as Mr Hudson's just told Mrs Bridges. His Majesty dining at Eaton Place. How about that!'

'Oh, that's nothing,' Clem said, waving it airily away with a hand. 'We've got Mr Micklewight of Micklewight's Sweets in Nottingham coming to dinner next week. And breakfast. And lunch. For five days. And there'll be three others with him. Each wanting a room apiece. And all wanting full board.'

'Gee!' Shelly said. 'Christmas has come early.'

'Christmas, Shelly,' Clem told her, 'has come just in time, going through the bills again earlier. Especially the utility ones. We were in danger of losing both electricity and the phone.'

'You know, I think perhaps I ought to be moving on,' Rupert said.

'You'll do no such thing!' Clem and Shelly said almost as one.

'You've already banished yourself to under the roof,' Clem added, referring to the top-floor singles that used to be maids' rooms and that were let at a reduced rate. Or in Rupert's case no rate at all.

'And you might well need that room as well soon,' Rupert said, 'coming up to Christmas. If you—'

Clem shot out a hand, forefinger pointed at him. 'You're staying,' she said, putting an end to the matter.

'Hey! But, honey – that's great,' Humphrey said, after coming up with a smile to go with it, hope disappearing almost as soon as it had arrived.

It wasn't that he had forgotten about the utility bills, it was that, as far as he was concerned, everything else took second place to the promise of a sackful of toys. For him it was about much more than money, than confessing to the matron that he couldn't afford it. He didn't care enough about the stuff to be embarrassed about the lack of it. It was about children and Christmas and toys, and a memory of his own meagre Christmas mornings, with plenty of love, but little money.

In his mind it would be as if he were denying Christmas. And because it was about Christmas, it allowed him to believe that something would turn up.

Chapter Three

When Humphrey spotted through the kitchen window that a blue minibus had pulled into the forecourt, he went out, welcome grin ready, to greet the four booked guests.

The driver, middle-aged in grey flannels creased with sitting and with a regimental badge on the breast pocket of his blazer, was standing by the driver's door stretching his lanky length from the knees up, in sections.

He regarded Humphrey lugubriously from under the plastic peak of his company hat.

'They're not here, mate.'

'Not here?' Humphrey echoed, peering in through the windows of the bus, seeing in its empty seats Christmas with no electricity and the phone unable to ring.

'They got out at the valley turn-off to walk the rest of the way.' He nodded at Humphrey, as if knowing Humphrey would have guessed the rest. 'His doing of course.'

'Who?' Humphrey said blankly.

'Gordon blinking Micklewight. Took over the sweet factory when his dad died recently. 'We're going on a journey,' he told 'em. And what a blinking journey it's been. Over three hours with him yacking about target agendas,

They were soaked from a downpour that had swept in over the hills of the valley, muddied from the arable fields it had softened and scratched by winter hedges, after following a series of short cuts, led by Gordon and his new compass.

But he had brought them there, he had delivered them from their own stormy sea.

'It is in challenge and adversity,' he said, finger lifted to emphasise another quote, when Charlotte brushed past him and took it out on one of the doors, wrenching it open and marching into the hall.

At the other end of the hall, under the sweep of the stairs, a log fire was burning.

She headed straight for it and stood, arms out to its heat, offering her damp clothes in a steamy embrace, while shivering extravagantly for Gordon's benefit.

'Ah, you got here!' Clem said, coming out of the kitchen. 'My word, the state of—'

'Yes, sorry about that,' Gordon said, indicating the mud on the flagged floor of the hall. 'We had to cross a few—'

'Oh, don't worry about that, that will wash off – I meant you, you poor things!'

'And I had my hair done yesterday. The new wedge cut,' Charlotte said, sharing her despair with another woman, a hand fluttering above her head indicating what once had been.

Clem, who had no idea what a wedge cut was, smiled in vague sympathy at hair flattened by Welsh rain.

'Well, the first thing we must do,' she said briskly, 'is to get you out of those wet clothes. Your rooms are ready. I'm on my own here at the moment. My husband's out in the shooting brake, looking for you. We were getting quite concerned.'

Gordon gave her one of his grins. 'Ah,' he said, 'that is kind of you, Lady Clementine. But—'

'Clem, please.'

'Clem. But there was really no need. We were on an exercise. Building team spirit. Forging links in the executive chain through challenge and adversity.'

'And led by Gordon here we have taken the first steps,' Terry Little, head of production said, getting it in before Keith and winning a smile of acknowledgement from Gordon.

'Most of them in the wrong direction,' Charlotte muttered.

'Well, anyway,' Clem said, 'if you wouldn't mind giving me a hand with the luggage. Then when you're ready we'll get you lunch. There's only two bathrooms, I'm afraid, but there's running water in your rooms. And we do have central heating.'

'Oh, bliss!' Charlotte said.

Chapter Five

What had once been the breakfast room on the first floor of the Hall had been turned into a bedroom, and all meals were now taken in the dining room on the ground floor, where the four guests the following day sat at breakfast.

Charlotte Taylor-Brown, head of marketing at Micklewight Sweets, and on a diet, was eating one of the prepared packets of muesli she'd brought with her. And boiled and scrambled eggs had been ordered, but Terry Little, who oversaw production at Micklewight's, had opted for the full English, winning Humphrey's approval.

And when Humphrey dropped in afterwards to see if more toast or tea or coffee was needed, Terry sat back, and as if finding breath for it, said, 'Delicious! I love sausages, and these…' He waved a hand at his empty plate, lost for words.

'Yeah, I know,' Humphrey said happily. 'I had them earlier. They're pork, from Stretch's, our butcher in Church Myddle. The back bacon's from there as well. Mr Stretch makes the sausages himself in his shop.'

Humphrey, enthused with a favourite subject, was about to tell him about the delights of the butcher's game pies, with particular emphasis on his favourite, pheasant crumble, and his beef and vegetable pasties, all baked to crusty perfection in a back-room oven, when Gordon, taking charge of the conversation said, as if delivering a verdict, 'Sir Humphrey, I like you.'

'Hey, Gord! I've told ya. Humph, please.'

'Humph,' Gordon said impatiently, getting the detail out of the way. 'Humph – I like you.'

'Well, great! Thank you,' Humphrey said, and chuckled vaguely.

'And do you like me, Humph?'

Gordon held out his hands, inviting him to take the next step.

'Well, yeah, you know. I mean…'

'Then say it, Humph. Say it,' Gordon urged, and grinned with a sudden brightness of teeth, a light showing him the way.

Humphrey glanced at the others, perfectly willing to join in if this was some sort of joke. But Charlotte had her head bent over the crossword in the *Telegraph* she'd ordered, and the attention of the two men was fixed on their leader, their eyes eager for the first truths of the day.

Humphrey moved his large head, grinned, chuckled again, and then got out, 'I like you, Gord.'

'Never be afraid of your feelings, Humph,' Gordon said gently. 'It's where you'll find yourself. Right? Am I right…?' he asked again, half teasingly, as Humphrey appeared to be arriving at the same conclusion.

'Well yeah, I guess you are, Gord,' Humphrey said, cheerfully obliging.

Gordon smiled. 'It's the journey that brought us here, Humph. To seek the truth of who we are. And to take that truth back with us to inspire others. Self-knowledge, inspiration, motivation, communication. Those are the banners we will lead our different teams under, into the future.'

'Yes!' Keith Rowe, pulled a punch in the air.

'And only the fittest will prosper there. Right, Gord?' Terry Little added, attempting the same sort of relish as Keith, but with a suggestion in it of appeal, as if seeking reassurance.

'Right, Tel!' Gordon said. 'And we,' he promised him, 'will be among them.'

'Yeah, that's right,' Terry said, sounding satisfied. 'And we'll be ready for it, thanks to you.'

Gordon lifted a finger. 'And that march into the future,' he said, pointing it at the ceiling, 'Humph, starts here. Under your very roof.'

'Among other things, Humph, see,' Terry said, sharing it with him, 'we'll be role playing, acting out the sort of scenarios we meet as department heads. To toughen our executive stance, you know?'

'I get ya, Tel,' Humphrey said, clearing away the plates.

'Another tool to help us dig down into who we are,' Gordon said. 'To find our own personal brand.'

'And inputting feedback afterwards with no holds barred,' Keith added, with relish.

'Sounds good to me, guys,' Humphrey said.

Not long after the breakfast things were cleared away, Shelly, on her way upstairs, stopped to answer the phone in the hall and took another booking, for the fifth guest bedroom. Batch Hall, for now, was full.

Something that Shelly, long under the influence of Jasmine Roberts, village psychic, had declared was an omen for better times to come.

The caller had said that he and his wife would arrive after lunch, and when they did so, Clem, while not in the least believing in it, decided that if it were an omen for better times to come, then she as lady of the house should be there to greet it.

'Very nice,' the man said after they'd arrived, entering and looking round the hall. 'Not considering selling by any chance, are you?'

Clem laughed, amused rather than affronted by it, from a stranger barely over the doorstep.

'No, I'm afraid not.'

'I'm in property development,' he went on, unabashed, taking in the carved Jacobean staircase, its treads worn with the centuries, and the oils up one side of it, the squires and their families in silk waistcoats and gowns, with lapdogs and fowling pieces in the manner of Gainsborough.

Had they been otherwise, had they carried the signature of the master, they would have gone under the hammer long before Humphrey and Clem moved in, leaving only the imprint of their frames to speak of the past, like the marks in the dining room where the last of the Stubbses had been.

'You'd be surprised at how many of the old families these days want it all taken off their hands, their options limited

38

and told her instead about the coat of arms, told it with the earnestness of a teacher, as if it were important she should know, while wanting to say something else to her, if not knowing what.

'Ah, I see. I like these old houses,' she said firmly, as if in defence of them. 'They're history, aren't they.'

'Yes, they are, Cindy,' Clem agreed.

Cindy smiled again, an older smile, more knowing, a smile learnt on the street, and with a flash of mischief glanced towards Mr Kirby and added, 'I like old things.'

Clem said that she'd get their key, and Mr Kirby followed her into the kitchen, running an eye like a tape measure over the large room.

Clem introduced him to Annie and Shelly.

'How many rooms in total here, Mrs – er—' Mr Kirby said.

'Clem,' Clem reminded him.

'Clem.'

'Do you know, we're really not sure,' she said, taking the key from the wall key cupboard. She did know, but didn't feel inclined to tell him.

Humphrey arrived then, looking for a hot drink with Rupert, who'd taken time off from the fields to help him clear out roof gutters after the gales of autumn.

Clem got as far as introducing Mr Kirby when Humphrey shot out a meaty hand, welcoming their new source of income. 'I'm Humph,' he said, slapping his arm. 'And this here's a friend of ours, Rupert.'

'And I'm Tony,' Mr Kirby said, grinning back. 'I was just saying to your lady wife, Humph. You two have a fortune tied up in this house. Pity you're not interested in selling.'

'Whaddya mean, a fortune?' Humphrey said alertly.

'I told Mr Kirby—' Clem started.

'Tony, please.'

'I told Tony that we're not thinking of selling.'

'Yeah, but what does he mean, a fortune?'

Mr Kirby told him what he had told Clem.

'The market for these old country piles has never been better. We have just completed through our agent here buying a similar property to yours in Llandiff,' he said, saying the name as it was written.

'Clandiff,' Annie put in, correcting an Englishman's pronunciation.

'Quite right, love,' Mr Kirby said with the ease of a salesman. 'And buying it, like all our acquisitions, under the tightest secrecy. The locals know nothing about it until the builders move in and turn it into something else,' he said with a chuckle. And then, about to mention money, sobered. 'And, as I said, we pay a good price – above current market value. We realise,' he added on a sententious note, 'that we are buying more than just bricks and mortar.'

'I've already told Mr— Tony,' Clem said, managing to make 'Tony' sound as formal as 'Mr', 'that we're not interested.'

'Yeah, that's right,' Humphrey said, in an interested sort of way, something that did not go unnoticed by Mr Kirby, who grinned again at him.

'And my husband would be even less likely to sell,' Clem said. She knew there would be no point in explaining why, but added a short polite laugh to soften it, while looking at Humphrey as if amused by his potential obstinacy.

'I'll show you to your room,' she said then, including Cindy in it, who was standing patiently in the doorway with the indifference of a taxi driver waiting to be paid.

Chapter Six

By Thursday afternoon of that week, the journey Gordon was leading them on in the bigger of the four booked bedrooms, his, could be heard all over the Hall, when Keith and Terry, after more of Keith's feedback with no holds barred, almost came to blows, and Charlotte left for her own bedroom, screaming with rage and banging doors, and then refusing to come out.

And early that evening, after Terry had phoned his wife and lied to her about how well he was doing in the team bonding exercises, he was sitting morosely at the bar in the lounge of the Steamer Inn when Phineas Cook came in.

Phineas, who had met Terry before in the pub, asked him when he was ordering his own drink if he'd like one. The other man indicated the glass on the bar in front of him, and morosely declined.

'Hard day?'

Terry's look said that Phineas didn't know the half of it.

'Diagnosing and facilitating team development.'

'I see,' Phineas said vaguely.

'Role playing in other words. Gordon – have you met Gordon?'

myself. But did I hear you right – you chalked up two forty not out?'

'Yes, that's right.'

'And how many sixes in one over?'

'Four,' Terry said, as if embarrassed by it now, a modest man who'd talked himself into a corner.

'Four sixes out of six balls,' Phineas said with a sort of wonder. 'And one of them over the pavilion roof.'

'And two hundred and forty on the board when I walked in,' Terry said, as if reminding him of the crime and asking for it to be taken into consideration.

'Walked in?' Phineas said indignantly. 'My dear chap, you should have been carried in, Terry. And hung with garlands. A hero come home. A knight from England's heart of Sunday cricket, his blade cut from the sacred *Salix alba caerulea*, the hallowed willow. An hour to play and the last men in, when twenty were needed for victory and five wickets still to fall. What's that you're drinking?'

'What?' Terry looked startled. 'It's – er – it's Black Boy bitter, half of bitter. But I—'

'Half of bitter! That's no drink for a hero. Allow me the honour. Patrick!' Phineas bawled, banging on the counter and trying to peer round into the public bar.

'That is the only libation worthy of a visitor from Olympus,' he said to Terry, indicating his own pint glass, before seeing off the last of the contents. 'Sheepsnout cider, nectar of the gods. Concocted up in the hills here by a white witch called Dotty Snape. A sorceress of the apple orchards, an alchemist among the barrels. A draught that owes more to Merlin and words said at midnight than to ladders and a press. As you're about to experience. Patrick!' he shouted again.

A shout that this time produced Patrick the landlord, breaking off a conversation in the public bar, and looking pained.

'Phineas…?' he enquired, his mild politeness a rebuke.

Patrick looked more bank manager than publican, a triangle of pressed white handkerchief poking up like a tongue from the breast pocket of a dark business suit, and a neat, tight-looking tie knot, like a comment on the general looseness of some of his customers. His eyes, behind black horn-rimmed glasses, those of a man who, like a bank manager at his desk, had viewed with professional detachment from behind his counter much human folly and indulgence.

A bank manager who showed reservations about the state of Phineas's account when Phineas ordered a round and told him to put it on his slate.

'I haven't reached my limit yet,' Phineas told him, waving him away to get on with it.

Patrick checked the red school exercise book of credit kept behind the bar, before picking up Terry's glass. 'Same again, sir?'

'No, no, Patrick,' Phineas said, 'not the same again. Is half of bitter the drink of the gods? Sheepsnout, man, Sheepsnout. Two pints if you please, Boniface, and whatever you're drinking. And something for Dilly if she's around,' he added, referring to Patrick's wife. 'There is greatness to celebrate.'

'She's not here. It's her night for yoga,' Patrick said, stooping to the barrel behind the bar, the name stencilled on its wood like a warning.

'Sheepsnout, the grape of Batch Valley,' Phineas told Terry. 'The wine, as the Welsh, whose door is never shut, put it, of our welcome. The gold that Dotty Snape's alchemy turns the humble apple into. You must not leave this valley, sir, without first tasting it. I, we, insist on it. It is your right.'

'Thank you,' Terry said doubtfully.

Patrick put the two pints on the counter, the cider moving in them like sunlight on shallows.

'She goes with that Sandra, the dentist's wife, to Kingham,' he said, entering the round neatly in the exercise book. 'They have it in the school there, in the gymnasium.'

'Who does?' Phineas said.

'Dilly. For the yoga class. It's more a social thing, if you ask me. Dilly looks up to her because her husband's a dentist. The same as—'

'Patrick!' Phineas broke in, impatient of anything but cricket, aiming a finger at Terry. 'This chap here, sitting there as if one of us, a mere mortal, is a god in human form,' he said, and while Terry shifted uneasily on his stool, he told Patrick why.

'My word,' Patrick said, looking at Terry as if about to ask for his autograph.

'And,' Phineas added, 'he sent one of those sixes clean over the pavilion roof.'

'My word,' Patrick said.

'Patrick here,' Phineas said to Terry, 'turns out for Batch Magna as an umpire. A man who sleeps with a copy of *Wisden* under his pillow. He *knows*. You have fallen, Terry, among your fellows.'

More rounds followed between the three men, Patrick taking his turn with drinks on the house, no longer a bank manager, not even a publican, with his wife out and a hero of the crease under his roof, but a Sunday cricketer. Forgetting half the time to open the exercise book, milking the gin optic for his own drink, his tie, bearing the dark gold and Trafalgar blue of the Batch Magna eleven, loosened.

Their talk was of summer, and the chop of leather on oiled yellow, talk of triumphs of the bat and defeats met out on the field, and heroic struggles on long, murmuring afternoons when the shadows lengthened and the midges swarmed, and twenty were needed for victory and five wickets still to fall.

When Terry finally left the Steamer Inn he left one of his colleagues, Charlotte Taylor-Browne, behind, drinking white wine, her diet forgotten, talking to Phineas at the bar, or rather listening to him talk. Doing so with an expression that suggested that if she'd heard it all before then she didn't in the least mind hearing it again. Phineas's blue eyes twinkling a sort of innocent mischief at her, as if inviting her, mischievously, to play.

And when Terry left he was no longer the weak link in Gordon's executive chain, but a giant again among Sunday cricketers. Marching back to Batch Hall fuelled by Sheepsnout and to the tune of a standing ovation following him into the pavilion on that golden Sunday afternoon. That time when much else apart from two hundred and forty not out was possible. A time when the future didn't wait like a threat. The time when, with a young family, he confidently applied for and got the job at Micklewight Sweets as head of production, and why.

In the Hall he poked his head into the residents' lounge and bar, where Gordon usually watched the late news on television with an air of being brought up to date on world affairs.

There was only Keith Rowe in there, sitting in front of the set with a brown ale and his shirtsleeves rolled up to his biceps.

Gordon had gone to fetch his cocoa, he said, and asked if he could help, doing so in a sort of triumphant mocking way, as if letting him know that there was now little difference in the executive chain between him and Gordon.

Terry surprised himself, as well as Keith, by saying that he wanted the organ grinder not his monkey. And then when Gordon appeared and with a show of teeth started talking about how they'd meant to get to the pub as it was the last night, Terry cut him short by tendering his resignation.

'I'm afraid I no longer have faith in the future of Micklewight Sweets,' the new Terry, or perhaps the old one back, said briskly. 'When your father took me on as production head—'

'Terry,' Gordon said, 'that was twenty-five years ago. That was the past,' he said, as if he both understood the error and forgave it, and showed his teeth as if about to lead him back to the right path.

'When he took me on as production head,' Terry

continued firmly, 'he did so because of my work in production at Pellhams, which included industrial relations. We kept the machines running, while elsewhere they had picket lines on the gate – and we did it through negotiation, Gordon, through sitting down and talking.'

'Yackety-yak,' Keith put in from his chair. 'The world's moved on since then, chum. That's the past and we're the future. And the future means business,' he added, borrowing a quote that Gordon had brought back with him from his own course on inspirational leadership.

'As far as my department is concerned, the future I've been learning about here is why Grant-Marker Accessories had a mass walkout a couple of months back,' Terry said. 'It just doesn't work, Gordon. All this gobbledegook nonsense may not matter when it comes to sales and marketing, but it does when it comes to production. And it's production that pays all our wages.'

'You've heard of breaking eggs and omelettes, Terry, haven't you?' Keith said. 'It's called taking charge, mate. As you don't seem to have been listening to what Gordon's been telling us.'

'No, Keith, I don't think Tel—' Gordon started.

'A proactive engine for change and increased output,' Keith steamed on, in the grip of the latest thinking and late-night reading. 'It's the future speaking, matey, the language of streamlined thinking, data mining models, key performance indicators, business metrics and analytics, process modelling and data integration…'

Terry quietly closed the door on it.

'You're a young man, Gordon,' he said. 'You have

time to learn. And I suggest you start. Before you steer Micklewight Sweets onto the rocks with all this nonsense. My resignation is effective from Monday. Goodnight to you,' Terry said, and headed for the stairs, mounting them with slow, deliberate steps, feeling suddenly in need of his bed.

The next morning, when it was still dark, Charlotte Taylor-Browne left the bedroom of the *Cluny Belle*, closing the door quietly behind her on a sleeping Phineas, the smell of the French cigarettes he smoked lingering with the stove smell in the sitting room. She was startled by the sudden screech of a barn owl from the opposite riverbank, the silence left behind louder to her city ears than any street noise.

She switched on the light. Phineas's dog Bill Sikes, who'd followed them from the pub last night, was lying on a sofa in front of the now dead pot-bellied stove in the centre of the room, its chimney fed into the paddler's original funnel, as if when lit she was once more making smoke, as if free after all these years from the ropes that held her there, tied to the land.

Sikes opened an eye briefly in her direction before closing it again. Whatever the world was getting up to at that hour it was none of his business.

Last night she had seen only romance. A paddle steamer moored under the moon, the two brass underway lamps from the *Belle*'s working days burning on deck stanchions, green for starboard, red for port.

'Bows into the storm and keep the wardroom open,' Phineas had said.

They had drunk wine and talked on the sofa, draped in a long rabbity Afghan coat from his hippy days, waiting for the coal he'd fed the stove to take. She told him about a recent failed relationship, and he told her that he hadn't been able to get it right either, and had three marriages in his past to prove it.

'What happened?' she'd asked.

'I did, according to them,' he told her. 'And taking now, one hopes, a more adult view of things, I have to say that they had a point. I'm a romantic, I quite see that now. And like all romantics I wrote my own love story. Misunderstandings, my dear Charlotte, were *bound* to follow.'

All in a different room, it seemed to her, to the cramped and untidy living space she saw now, smelling of the river and with a chill from it now that the stove was out. There were used mugs and glasses sitting about, and a plate with congealed bits of egg on it from yesterday's breakfast on the table in front of the stove, and above it, hanging on a string arrangement, a selection of his underwear waiting to be put away.

She had used the lavatory in the stern of the boat last night, the heads, as he called it, and on a wall was a photograph of a very young, floppy-haired Phineas as a member of a cricket team. It was a school photograph, he'd told her, taken when he'd represented Eton in an under-sixteen team.

Charlotte knew about Eton. The winners went there. The movers and shakers. Captains of industry, generals and admirals and bishops went there, high court judges and prime ministers and other leading politicians, the aristocracy and even royalty went there. And then there

DC Chambers went to work on the two suitcases, and then the two chests of drawers and the double wardrobe, before running out of things to dust.

'Nothing. Somebody's wiped up after themselves,' he said, putting his kit away, science having been frustrated, along with DC Chambers on his first professional outing.

'So we're looking at an inside job or a sneak thief,' the sergeant said.

Before they went back downstairs Mr Kirby took the sergeant aside, and passed on what Annie, chattily, had told him about Rupert, how he came to be there.

The sergeant digested it. 'Well, doesn't of course mean he's a thief as well. Could he have known where you had the money?'

'No. As I said, nobody knew.'

'Not even your wife?'

'No, I don't think she did – but what are you suggesting?'

'Not suggesting anything, just—'

'My wife's got her own money, she doesn't need mine,' he said, even managing a laugh at the idea, anxious to lead the sergeant away from it, from the possibility of a scandal and its effects on his business relationship with the investment bankers. And if his real wife found out she'd do the rest, leave him this time, and strip him to the bone on the way out. 'No, I think this Rupert bloke has got to be worth looking into.'

'Well,' Sergeant Bevin said, 'it's not as if we're spoilt for suspects.'

Back in the kitchen the sergeant said he wanted to go over where everyone was during the time Mrs Kirby was out of their room. And when he got to Humphrey and

Rupert he asked if either of them had left the gatehouse at any time. They said they hadn't.

And then Rupert remembered that he had, remembered it with a sort of eagerness, wanting to please. He had to walk up to the Hall, he said, to use the lavatory, as the gatehouse wasn't yet plumbed in.

'Oh, yeah, that's right,' Humphrey agreed. 'I'd forgotten about that.'

'You're Mr...?' Sergeant Bevin said.

'Ainsworth. Rupert Ainsworth. I had a second Christian name but I'm afraid I'm not sure I remember it.'

'That's all right, sir,' Sergeant Bevin said, the last remark an oddity which aroused more interest in him. 'And around what time would that be when you paid your visit here?'

Rupert had no idea, and it disturbed him in this serious business that he didn't. Time no longer meant for him what it meant for the sergeant, or anyone else in that room. Time for as long as he could remember was always elsewhere, in the world he walked through each year, in homes and offices and factories, and carried about on wrists. A world he had walked away from once and which he now felt trapped in again, the room too full, their world suddenly too much there.

The winter society of the spikes was not the same thing at all. Even in the communal kitchens most men were apart, alone with what had brought them there. The punished faces of lives recklessly lived, the unlucky ones still trying to work out what had happened, how things could have gone that wrong. The quietly mad, their own thoughts keeping them company, and those who, even when joining in a conversation, even when starting one, almost always with him to succeed, so that he didn't always have to be looking on, another loser at the feast, she had lied.

His father, who had earned no more than that needed to live on, had never been any sort of businessman. He had never cared enough about money to get that bored.

And Humphrey knew then that what he was doing by moving into Batch Hall, its past there in near ruins. By ignoring all the sound reasons why he shouldn't, and the chance to succeed in business at last, by turning the place in an olde worlde English theme park, was what his father, his real father, would have done.

So, as he saw it, they were doing it together.

That Sunday for Humphrey was an oasis reached, and tomorrow another day. Another day and the start of another week, one nearer to Christmas. But this was Sunday, and he gave praise to it with his neighbours, sang to it with all his heart, all his gratitude, lifting his voice up to the ancient carved timbers of a Norman roof, and was restored.

Chapter Eleven

The following Monday, it did not go unnoticed by the female passengers she would normally have spent the journey gossiping with downstairs, that Miss Wyndham, this time, was not alone when she boarded the Kingham bus from Batch Magna.

She and Rupert went upstairs so that Rupert could smoke his pipe. Leaving the tall star-shaped chimneys of Batch Hall behind, and his bedroom, one of the small rooms under the roof where once the female servants had climbed each night like roosting birds, and the three houseboats on the river, smoke like breath in the chilled air from their winter stoves.

Past the ruins of Batch Castle on a hill above the river, a fortress once against border incursions and the forces of Cromwell, a past through which the wind now blows. And the fields where he was planting new life to rise again to meet the spring, and small black and white farms among orchards, the apple trees mulched and lagged for winter, out under the wooded hills of the valley, the bare trees flowering like cracks against a pale winter sky.

Chapter Twelve

Miss Wyndham saw someone she recognised, looking in the window of a jeweller's. It was Cindy Kirby. She had been introduced to her when talking to Annie Owen outside the village shop on Thursday as Cindy was going in.

'Wait, Rupert!' she said, startling him by pulling him into the doorway of a chemist's shop, and then putting her head out cautiously to peer round, narrow-eyed, at the jeweller's, a woman given to intrigue.

'What is it? What's wrong?' Rupert said, as if wondering after Saturday what was coming next.

'Didn't you see her?'

'Who?' Rupert said.

'Mrs Kirby,' Miss Wyndham said, keeping an eye on her. 'Not that Clem thinks that – she's going in!' she said, watching her disappearing into the shop. 'She's going into Grant's the jeweller's. Presumably to buy something.'

'Well what of it, Harriet?' Rupert said, after opening the door of the chemist's for a woman, doffing his hat to her.

'Because Grant's is not cheap. And she complained to Annie about not having money, that he, Mr Kirby, kept her short. So I find that very curious, very curious indeed,'

Miss Wyndham said, more to herself, mulling over the evidence.

They waited, Rupert opening the door for more customers, and then Miss Wyndham said, 'She's leaving. Careful!' she added, pulling her head back. 'She's coming this way. Quick! Into the shop,' she said, pushing him towards the door, Rupert opening it again, almost out of habit now, and for Miss Wyndham this time, before following her.

'She's coming in!' Miss Wyndham said, glancing back through the glazed door. 'Come on,' she said, dragging him over to shelves of bathroom accessories.

'Don't just stand there, Rupert,' she hissed, 'pretend to be looking at something. The shampoos,' she suggested, and out of the corner of an eye saw Cindy walk past and stop at a cosmetics stand further along.

'Come on!' she said, dragging him back to the door. 'We're going in,' she said, out on the street.

'Going in where?' he almost wailed.

'The jeweller's of course. Now, Rupert, listen,' she said, linking an arm through his and walking him along. 'You're my husband, and Cindy... Cindy is a neighbour's girl. We saw her leaving your shop, we'll say, and – er—'

She paused at an estate agent's to think, staring unseeing at this week's desirable properties.

'It's her birthday! Yes, that's it, it's her birthday tomorrow.'

'Whose? Whose birthday?' Rupert said, as if appealing to her.

Miss Wyndham smiled at him in a kindly way. 'Cindy's,' she said. 'Our neighbour's girl.'

Rupert shook his head. 'I'm afraid I don't understand.'

'It's not his money, it's mine!' she burst out petulantly. 'It's what he owes me. And he wasn't gonna pay, I knew that. It's not his money, it's mine!'

'The court won't see it that way.'

'I wasn't gonna let your friend stand still for it,' Cindy said to Miss Wyndham. 'Honest. I like him. He's a nice old geezer. I was gonna write a letter. And the pendant isn't for me, it's not my style. It's for a friend of mine, Kay. She's got a hairdresser's in Essex, and she can give me a job. I've done hairdressing, done colouring. And she'll put me up as well, till I can get a place. That's what I needed the rest of the money for. The pendant was a present for Kay. For Christmas,' Cindy added into the silence that followed her speech.

'What about your family, child?' Miss Wyndham said, surprising herself by going to her, sitting on the bed with her.

Cindy shook her head, her expression telling Miss Wyndham all she cared to know about her family.

'I see,' was all Miss Wyndham said.

'How were you going to get to Essex?' Clem asked.

'By train. I was gonna hitch a lift to Shrewsbury, if I couldn't get a bus.'

'There's a railway station at Church Myddle,' Miss Wyndham said. 'Much nearer.'

Clem came to a decision. 'What time is Mr Kirby due back?'

'Dunno. Could be any time.'

'Right. Pack your suitcase. I'll see what trains there are from Church Myddle. Where in Essex is your friend?'

'Brentwood. Can I keep the money then?'

'Well, as you say, it's yours. I'm sure you earned it,' Clem said, before realising what she had said.

'Well, not really,' Cindy said, taking the remark professionally. 'He's got problems down there.'

'Yes, well,' Clem said, 'I'll make that phone call.'

'But what about the old man, what about Rupert?' Cindy said, when Clem disappeared.

'I'm afraid I rather exaggerated the situation,' Miss Wyndham told her. 'The charge to all and intents and purposes has been dropped. I can tell you, my dear, that I have it from Clem, always a reliable source, that it's also unlikely that Mr Kirby will be pursuing it. Mr Kirby, one gathers, has other problems, apart from those down there,' Miss Wyndham added to Cindy's surprise.

When Clem returned she had a sheet of paper from the notebook kept by the phone in the hall, and a plastic bag with palm trees and a beach under a lurid sun and 'California' written across the bottom of it. 'This was left behind by one of our American visitors.'

'Ohh, I like that,' Cindy said.

'I thought you might. I've put crisps and a couple of packets of Shropshire Dunk biscuits in it. You can put your magazines in there as well, and that ghastly drink you insist on rotting your stomach with. It's a long journey, nearly four hours. There's a train from Church Myddle in just over an hour. You change at Shrewsbury, and there's a couple of changes after that. I've written it all down for you,' she said, giving her the sheet of paper.

'Can I get a bus?'

'I doubt that would be necessary, even if you could get one in time,' Miss Wyndham said.

'I'll take you in the shooting brake,' Clem said. 'There's room in that to duck down if we encounter Mr Kirby's car on the road.'

Cindy looked at them. 'Thank you. Thank you both,' she said tearfully.

She hugged them in turn, holding on to them and snivelling, Miss Wyndham tentatively putting her arms around her, holding her in a stiff, awkward embrace.

Miss Wyndham was still sitting on the bed after they had left the room, after Clem had stopped off briefly in the kitchen, after they had driven away, the sound of the brake fading.

As with Rupert, sometimes the world was too much with her, the distance she had long kept from it crossed in a couple of strides with a hug from a young woman who might have been a granddaughter, a world of things that weren't and now could never be.

Chapter Thirteen

Phineas Cook was rich, courtesy of his publisher and Royal Mail, or Post Brenhinol, as Dyfan Lewis, postman from the Welsh half of the village, insisted.

Phineas didn't care what it was called. It had delivered on Saturday morning to his doormat on the *Cluny Belle* a royalty cheque, earned in the name of his alter ego Warren Chase, author of hard-bitten detective novels.

He had been surprised, even thinking it a mistake, when a publisher had accepted his first book. He was tempted to ask why, but didn't because he needed the money, and thought it might draw their attention to what he considered to be the sheer comic-book tosh of the doings of his Scotland Yard detective, Inspector MacNail.

He had only started writing in the first place after reading what he thought was even worse tosh in Kingham Library. And when he received the publisher's thrice-yearly royalty cheques, he did so with the same sort of surprise, and not without a little guilt, as if they were the result of begging letters he'd been sending to people.

With Bill Sikes trotting along with him, and dressed in a clean shirt, flannels that could have done with an iron under his Afghan, and with a bright red and white spotted kerchief round his neck, to go with a morning that suddenly had a holiday air to it, he had arrived not more than ten minutes after the Steamer Inn had opened to cash his cheque.

'Take a port and lemon for madam out of it,' he told Patrick, a drink for Annie Owen, waylaid when on her way back from the village shop to the *Felicity H*. 'A pint of your finest Black Boy bitter for me, Patrick, m'dear, and whatever you're having. And discharge, if you will, landlord, my slate.'

He turned to Annie. 'Wouldn't it be marvellous, Annie, if we could have life, all the awkward bits, on the slate? All our mistakes and follies written in chalk, to be wiped clean after a certain time, allowing us to start again. Your health, old thing,' he added, handing her the port and lemon.

'Thank you, lovey. And yours.'

Annie settled with her shopping at a table, while Phineas, lordly with money, used the pub phone to ring Annie's husband, Owain, to tell him to get himself up there. Feeling it had the making of a jolly, he then rang Priny and her husband, the Commander, and Jasmine Roberts on the *Cluny Queen*.

Jasmine, a single mother, and a woman wide ranging and generous with her favours, lived on the houseboat with her large family. No one knew quite how many that meant, not even Jasmine it seemed at times, but she turned up with a small gang of the youngest, who were fed pop and crisps by Phineas to keep them quiet.

Clem and Shelly were out on a sandwich run when he phoned the Hall, and Rupert, the case against him dropped entirely, as the solicitor had predicted it would be, was working in the silence of the fields, and the freedom of being alone.

But Humphrey was there, and after muttering unconvincingly about having things to do, was now sharing a table with the others overlooking the pub terrace, with its summer chairs and tables, the sunshades furled for winter, and the upended mahogany sculling boats for hire on the slipway below for the tourists who hardly ever came, and the river.

Humphrey, nursing a martyred half of Black Boy, instead of his usual pint, mentioned the empty bedrooms at the Hall, now Mr Kirby had departed, and the lack of bookings, his thoughts, as they never were for long lately, not untouched by that of a children's hospital ward and a promised sack of Christmas toys.

'You want a few Yanks, Humph. A few rich American tourists, boy,' Owain suggested, ignoring, or forgetting, that Humphrey was an American, so much now was he of this place.

The Commander, feeding the last of a packet of pork scratchings to Bill Sikes and the Cunninghams' Welsh collie, Stringbag, under the table, said, 'They need, Owain, guests of any stripe, any colour or tongue. Americans, Canadians, Australians, New Zealanders, Italians… Jamaicans…' The Commander appeared to run out of countries.

'Hungarians, Egyptians, Fijians, Tahitians, Malaysians, Tunisians,' his wife said, helping him out, before breaking off to giggle about it with Annie.

'And Martians,' Annie got out.

The Commander's voice rose above it. 'I was merely pointing out that it matters not to the Hall what nationality their guests are.'

'But the Yanks spend money everywhere,' Owain pointed out.

'If by everywhere, Owain, you mean the village shop and the pub, how the devil is that going to help the Hall?' the Commander wanted to know testily, moving in his seat, his gammy leg reminding him it was there. It was the legacy of an accident on his aircraft carrier during the war, his breast when he skippered a summer PS *Batch Castle* in the uniform of a shipping master, bright with Fleet Air Arm medal ribbons.

The *Castle* had once been another houseboat, his home and Priny's, and when she had developed arthritis, not improved by sitting on water, Humphrey had suggested a straight swap for one of the old Masters' Cottages on the river. The boat was then converted back to a working paddle steamer, her whistle heard once more in the valley on summer mornings, her deck busy again with people.

The wartime accident had also cost the Commander an eye, and he had commissioned a miniaturist to paint a collection of plain glass ones, depicting naval victories and landscapes that spoke of England.

He favoured Humphrey with his good one. In the other, Turner's *Sunrise* in miniature went up in yellow flames over Norham Castle.

'You need a ghost, Humphrey,' he pronounced. 'The Americans expect it in a house of that age and history.'

'Ah, come round to my way of thinking now have you, about Americans?' Owain said, chuckling and sharing it with the others.

'I confess I must have missed your mention of ghosts at the time, Owain.'

'That's because I didn't make one.'

'Then what the devil—'

'They're right about ghosts, Humph,' Phineas broke in. 'I've just remembered. I read a piece some time back about one in a bed and breakfast establishment in Pinner. Walking about at midnight with his head under an arm. The story got out and they ended up having to turn business away.'

Humphrey took in that happy state of affairs for a moment, and then said, 'Yeah, well, we don't have a ghost. With or without its head.'

'Course you do, Humph!' Jasmine said with a small laugh of surprise. She had returned from the bar with armfuls of crisps for her brood playing on the floor, walking among them and feeding them from the bags like chickens.

'Saw one in August, I did,' Jasmine went on, sitting down again to her pint of cider. 'When you had that party. A young housemaid, in an apron. Happy, she was. Tripping up the backstairs, in love if ever I saw it. Face like a flower, opened to love like the sun,' Jasmine said, more to herself.

'Ohh, there's nice,' Annie said.

'And what were you doing on the backstairs?' Priny wanted to know, knowing full well what she was doing on the backstairs.

'I got lost, me,' Jasmine said indignantly.

'You didn't say anything about any ghost at the time,' Humphrey said.

'Well, I didn't like to. You know, in front of people.'

'Well, there you are, Humph,' the Commander said briskly. 'One ghost. Now all you need to do is—'

'Look, just because Jas saw a ghost don't mean everybody's gonna to see it,' Humphrey said, waving a hand at Jasmine, not only a psychic, but a world-famous one, according to her advertisements in the local press. 'And anyway, the paying guests don't use the backstairs.'

'Then say she was on the main staircase,' Owain said with Welsh guile. 'One of the family, see.'

'Descending in a lovely silk gown with petticoats and lots of ribbons,' Annie said.

'And cleavage,' Priny said, screwing a cigarette into a long amber holder. 'It's a social occasion and she's after a husband.'

'But nothing too obvious, Priny,' Annie said.

'No. No, just enough to catch the male eye. Quite right, Annie. I always did go overboard in that department. Comes of trying to make what little one had go further.'

'Well, whether below stairs or above, Humph, whether lady or scullion, you have a ghost,' the Commander said. 'So what are you waiting for, sir?'

'Yes, come along, Humph!' Phineas said. 'If a modest semi in Pinner can field a ghost, then surely Batch Hall, with four hundred years of history—'

'Look, I appreciate what you're trying to do here. But if we have a ghost then we haven't seen it. And we haven't seen it because there's no ghost to see! Or none for normal people to see,' he added, not wanting to hurt Jasmine's feelings.

Phineas leaned towards him across the table.

'Not yet there isn't. But that's not to say, old chap, that there won't be,' he said and, sitting back, beamed reassurance at him.

Chapter Fourteen

A couple of days after that, when Humphrey came in from the grounds after turning part of a dead tree into winter fuel, he found Phineas in the kitchen drinking tea with Annie Owen and Shelly.

'You'll never guess what, Humphie!' his mother said.

'What?' he said, looking suspiciously at Phineas.

He had seen that look in his eyes before. It was a visit from the world Phineas lived in half the time, a world and its possibilities that most adults had long stopped believing in. A world, he had no trouble remembering, Phineas had shared with him more than once before.

'We're going to have a ghost,' Shelly said.

'Artemus Strange,' Phineas told him, introducing him with a sweep of his hand.

'Found him in Kingham. In the reference library, he did,' Annie put in, as if Artemus had been missing. 'He was only eighteen, he was, when he died.'

'He was killed here, in this very house. In the Civil War – or the Rebellion, as Clem insists,' Phineas said. 'When Sir Richard, or just plain Richard as he was then, had garrisoned his Royalist supporters in Batch Castle.'

Humphrey sat down to listen despite himself. He'd read up on the Civil War for the summer Open Days, when he took groups of bemused-looking visitors on a tour of the Hall, pointing out its history in a Bronx accent, this ninth baronet of his line in a Hawaiian shirt and chewing on a cigar. His ancestor, the first baronet, Sir Richard Strange, who led the line of past squires in oils up one side of the main staircase, had been awarded the title for his allegiance to the king.

'A small troop of Horse carried on to here,' Phineas went on. 'Some of the servants fled through the grounds. Two of the male indoor staff were killed defending the front doors. Artemus shepherded his mother, Hawis, his three younger siblings, governess and the cook into what was then the schoolroom upstairs.'

'He told them to barricade themselves in,' Shelly said, her eyes full of the deed. 'While he stood on the other side of the door, sword in hand, ready to defend them. A true hero, he was. And at eighteen not long out of the schoolroom himself.'

'He acquitted himself well,' Phineas said. 'Sending four of them on their way for God to deal with before he fell, wounded. The Captain of Horse, because Artemus was a gentleman, delivered the coup de grâce. Then Richard and his Royalists, the Ironheads having been put to the rout at Batch Castle, came to the rescue.'

'And Richard and his mother found their son dying,' Annie added, looking at Phineas, the source of that information, with a sort of anguish.

'Jeez!' Humphrey said. 'We didn't know anything about this. Well, I can sure use it on Open Days. But what a sad story.'

He sat shaking his head over it, and then looked at the teapot on the table. 'That just made, Annie?'

'No,' she said, getting up. 'I'll put the kettle on. We'll all have another.'

'Any Shropshire Dunks to go with it?'

'I got a new couple of packets,' his mother said. 'Can't run out of Shropshire Dunks.'

Phineas, losing Humphrey to Shropshire Dunk assorted biscuits, and knowing the romantic heart that beat beneath his formidable bulk, said, 'Another interesting historical detail, incidentally, that came to light was that the young governess was Artemus's sweetheart. His betrothed, actually.'

'Get away!' Annie said, sitting down again,

'Yes, apparently,' Phineas said casually, playing with his teaspoon.

'Who was the—?' Humphrey started.

'Hmm? Who, the governess? Oh, a girl from the Welsh side of things. The other side of Rhysoch, actually. The youngest daughter of a Welsh peer. It is said that Artemus died with her name on his lips.'

'Oh!' Annie cried, the sound wrung from her.

'Gave his last breath to their love,' Phineas added, gratified with her reaction.

'Gee, that is sad,' Shelly said.

Humphrey was shaking his head again at it.

'What was it?' he asked then.

'What was what?'

'Her name.'

Phineas thought about it. 'Brynna. That's it. Her name was Brynna.'

'Oh there's a coincidence,' Annie said. 'Same name as an old aunt of mine. It means woman from the hills. Mind you, she was from Swansea. No hills there, is there.'

'Ah, but there are the other side of Rhysoch, I'm led to believe.'

'Yes, well, I don't know that area,' Annie said.

'Oh, yes, there's lots of them there, apparently. A hilly sort of country. And an interesting footnote, incidentally, Humph, for your visitors. The meaning of the name. People like those sort of touches.'

'Yeah, I'll remember that, the next Open Day.'

'Not just Open Day, old man. But your paying guests as well. Those with an interest in the supernatural. Or those on your ghost tours. At – say – a fiver a punter. Have a look at what other people are charging. Clem will sort that out.'

'Ghost tours?'

'Very popular. "The Ghost of Artemus Strange", I can see it now.'

'They do a ghost tour at the Blue Boar in Shrewsbury,' Annie said. 'The restless spirit of a traveller murdered for his purse. Lots of people, they say, have seen him, and heard him, his screams. Had his throat cut, he did, in his bed.'

'Ah. Sound effects,' Phineas said. 'Nice detail. I'll look into it.'

'And here's another detail, Phin, while you're looking into things,' Humphrey said. 'We don't have a ghost.'

'Yes, we do. We've got Artemus!' Annie said, indignantly protective.

'I mean, we don't have an actual ghost, Annie. You know, one that people would pay money to look at. That kinda ghost.'

Phineas grinned slowly. 'Ah! And that, my dear fellow, is where you are wrong. Not wrong, I grant you, in the sense that there won't be an actual ghost, headless or otherwise, wandering the place. But wrong to think that Artemus cannot walk again, his sleep of centuries rudely disturbed. Something I'll come back to.'

'Could be all that banging and sawing, and that,' Annie suggested. 'When you had the schoolroom turned into a double bedroom in the summer. Enough to wake anybody.'

'Clem's idea,' Humphrey said. 'And a double that's still empty. And the bank still want their money back on the loan. We'd have been better off, as I said at the time, finishing the lodge with it and going into the self-catering lark. It's like the business conferences in the servants' hall we planned,' he grumbled on, 'and spent all that money advertising them in business magazines. And have we had a conference there yet? No, we haven't,' he said, answering his own question with some satisfaction.

Phineas leaned towards him. 'And it's that stuff, Humph, money, lucre, filthy or otherwise, that will be pouring in when Artemus Strange walks again, and his story, his gallant act that day, is given an airing in local and national prints, and picked up by radio and television, I wouldn't be at all surprised. Wouldn't surprise me in the *least*!'

'You mean someone pretending to be the ghost of Artemus?' Humphrey said.

'That essentially,' Phineas said slowly, as if it were rather more involved than that, 'would be the case, yes.'

Humphrey stared at him, in his expression the thought of money pouring in meeting his past experience of Phineas.

mind would be half of the highlight of the thing, and so must be an expert duellist with the rapier, the sword of the Cavalier. An artist who carves drama out of the air with its blade. A man who scorns the stairs for a chandelier or a shortcut over a banister, and who laughs in the face of overwhelming odds. The more the merrier, as far as he's concerned.'

'Sounds like Errol Flynn,' Annie said.

'He's dead,' Shelly said.

'But Rory O'Keefe is very much alive,' Phineas said. 'And at a loose end.'

'Who?' Humphrey said.

'Rory O'Keefe. Star of stage, screen and television. Recently played a lance corporal in *Rising Damp*. A brief part of few words but he triumphed in it. But far more important as far as this is concerned, he won an award for fencing at RADA. And has employed that skill in several period films since.'

'Oh,' Annie said. 'And he's Irish, is he, Phineas? Born there, I mean?'

'As Galway Bay, Annie. His home county in fact. He's Spanish dark, a legacy of the Armada – the Invincible Armada, until Drake and our weather taught it otherwise – limping in there on their way home, and some of them staying. Black hair and blue eyes. A devil of a fella.'

'Mmm,' Shelly murmured appreciatively.

'An Irish actor and Phineas Cook.' Clem mused doubtfully on the combination for a moment, and then said, 'I take it he is a friend of yours?'

'Of long standing. Goes back to my London days. We shared a house with others in Chelsea. Shared a house and many a hangover. Haven't seen him for ages, so, like me, no doubt he's grown up a bit since then.'

Clem ignored that last bit, and said, 'Well, whatever you have in mind, unless your friend is prepared to work for nothing—'

'Oh, but he is, Clem,' Phineas said. 'I've already discussed it with him, on the phone. Put out feelers, as it were. He thinks it great craic, as he put it.' He beamed, sharing it with the others at the table.

'Thinks what is great craic?' Clem said. 'Perhaps you wouldn't mind discussing it with us as well.'

'Right, well, the people who do the historical shows here in the summer.'

'The Civil War re-enactors,' Clem said. 'The English Revolution Society.'

'Whaddya want with them?' Humphrey said suspiciously, the summer shows they put on in Batch Castle and on the lawns of the Hall good sources of income for the estate.

'Well, my idea was to have a few from both sides of the argument, Roundheads and Cavaliers, replaying the famous incident when Artemus is cut down defending the womenfolk of the house. There's bound to be at least one good fencer among them. I don't mean their usual bashing and slashing, but really good fencers.'

'There's several,' Clem said. 'On both sides. Club fencers, doing it competitively.'

Phineas spread his hands. 'Well, there you are then. There should be no problem finding someone to give Rory a run as Captain of Horse. Because at the very end of the show they duel. The whole thing cannot *fail* to appeal. They'll be queuing up. I'd leave the financial arrangements with the re-enactors to you. I seek no reward. And Rory has his art.'

'And where would the ghost come in?' Humphrey wanted to know.

'The Ghost of Artemus Strange, as any advertising would read,' Phineas said, 'would be your second source of income. He'd appear after, say, three or four shows, alerted in his sleep in the other world. His spirit responding, as his earthly entity did, to the desperate cries of the womenfolk. And it occurred to me, incidentally, that with a little rehearsal the three ladies here might provide that chorus. Both in the re-enactment, and in ghostly wailing for Artemus's appearance. Three parts, ladies, not to be sniffed at. Absolutely indispensable. Like the witches in Macbeth – while not of course, let me say at once, being the least withered and wild, or remotely weird. Nor, let it be said, black and midnight hags. But just as essential to the plot. Anyway, the – er… Where was I?'

'The ghost of Artemus Strange appearing,' Shelly, who'd been following it avidly, said.

'Thank you, Shelly. The ghost of Artemus Strange is called forth, summoned by their distress. And as he did so bravely in life, engages with knightly chivalry the enemy. On his own. His only defence against a troop of Ironheads intent on rape and pillage, his courage and his rapier. All to the tune of a few quid a head when you do ghost tours. The sort that are coining it at the Blue Boar pub in Shrewsbury, by all accounts,' he said, and looked at Annie.

'Oh, that's right,' she said. 'Very popular they are, too. We were going last week, Bryony and me. But they were full on that night.'

'And how much will this Irish Errol Flynn charge for his Richard?' Clem wanted to know.

Phineas leaned towards her to deliver the news. 'Nothing, Clem. Not a penny. You'd offend him if you offered.'

'Why?' she said.

'Yeah, why?' Humphrey said. 'Not on the run, is he, and looking for somewhere to hole up?'

Phineas looked both disappointed and hurt. 'Not only do you look a gift horse in the mouth, you want a criminal check run on it.'

Humphrey put his hands up, as if in surrendering to that look. 'OK, OK, I was joking.'

'Rory,' Phineas went on patiently, 'is what the acting profession call "resting" at present.'

'Out of work,' Clem said.

'Between jobs. The acting professional looks at things rather more optimistically. And as well as finding the idea appealing, for him, with a reasonable cheque yet untapped from his last film job, there would also be the chance to get away for a while from the temptations of London. Like me, he's decided to take a more mature approach to his finances.'

'I seem to have heard that one before,' Annie said.

There was a silence. Humphrey and Clem looked at each other.

Humphrey shrugged. 'Well, I guess so. I mean, what have we got to lose?'

'Yes, I agree,' Clem said. 'And Artemus deserves it. Deserves to have his bravery more widely known.'

Phineas slapped the table. 'Splendid! I'll sort out train times with him, and arrange to pick him up. What fun!'

'Doesn't he have a car?' Humphrey said.

'He doesn't see the point, living in London. And besides, he likes a drink.'

'I see,' Clem said doubtfully. 'And where do you see this happening, Phineas? I mean, there's not a lot of room—'

'Yes, I know, Clem. I've been giving that some thought. And I think the bedroom directly facing the top of the stairs should stand for the schoolroom. And our audience could sort of stand on the stairs and the half-landing. We could get, what? Say twenty? Yes, twenty. We could accommodate that number comfortably.' Phineas shared a confident smile with them.

'How long they gonna stand there for?' Humphrey wanted to know.

'Oh, I don't know. Forty-five minutes perhaps. No longer I shouldn't think.'

'And we could give them a free coffee and a hotdog, take their minds off their feet,' Shelly suggested.

'Excellent idea, Shelly,' Phineas said.

'How many of each side do you have in mind?' Clem asked.

'As regards space, I think we could get away with five – which would include the Captain of Horse and Rory.'

Clem appeared to be considering it again.

'OK, I'll speak to Cuthbert Stanley,' she said then, referring to the man, a retired schoolteacher, who had founded and ran the re-enactment society. 'He'll sort out the two sides for us, and the Captain of Horse fencer.'

'We'll do Artemus proud, Clem. And all I ask on Rory's behalf is a bed under the roof here. My camp bed's broken and Sikes always bags the sofa, the bully.'

'Yeah, sure,' Humphrey said. 'He can have one of the doubles, if he wants. We can always move him upstairs if need be. Not that I see that happening before Christmas.'

'And he can eat with us,' Clem added.

Phineas smiled. 'Of course he can. And in anticipation of you agreeing to it, I had a word with Maggie yesterday. Maggie, yes?' he prompted when they looked blank. 'Wardrobe mistress at the Kingham Rep...?' he said with a touch of impatience, as if it should be obvious who he was referring to.

Oh, yes, they said vaguely. It was difficult to keep up with Phineas's girlfriends, each in turn introduced by him with hints that this one, this time, could be the one. And meaning it, this time.

'I gave her Rory's sizes, in case you did agree, and she told me that she can fix him up with a Cavalier uniform. And that we can have it for the foreseeable future – and the foreseeable future, my dears, extends well beyond the end of the pantomime season in February. And in that time, well, I mean, who knows what might have happened.'

Chapter Fifteen

Phineas's ghost was again being discussed in the Hall's kitchen, while Jasmine, in pursuit of the jackpot she was convinced was in the next spin of fruit, was playing one of the machines between the two large windows. The machine Phineas had been playing before leaving a few minutes ago, poorer than when he came in, despite his plan.

Jasmine also had a plan. It was to wait with a sort of studied casualness for whoever was playing the machines at the time to shorten the odds she'd read about somewhere, and then step in and collect the jackpot that had only just been missed.

It didn't work this time either. But given the shortening odds, the way Jasmine calculated it, ignoring the times she wasn't there to witness them shortening, perhaps in someone else's favour, it was only a matter of time.

Phineas's plan was even less logical than Jasmine's.

On his last gamble, he would always walk away immediately after spinning the reels, as if indifferent to the result. He was waiting for luck to astonish him, waiting for it to strike when he wasn't looking, the way he'd seen it happen in a film once. Waiting for a fabled year's worth of jackpots to arrive at once in a cascade of coins, and then, gasping with surprised delight, filling his pockets and stuffing them down his shirt front and into his Panama hat.

Leaving her oldest daughter Meredith in charge of the rest of the family, Jasmine was wearing jeans and wellington boots, instead of one of her usual silk dresses printed with the heavens, with stars and moons, golden sun faces and zodiac circles, but wearing her work jewellery, her crescent-and-hand necklace and Egyptian charm bracelets, her plump hands heavy with fish and abraxas rings.

She was on her way to a hill farm across the border in Gwen-y-Coed. The farmer, seeing her advertisement in a local newspaper, was taking advantage of her 'special rate for pets' to look at his collie who, almost overnight, had lost interest in anything to do with sheep. As far as the dog was concerned he had never seen them before, didn't care if he never saw them again, and meanwhile wanted nothing to do with them.

Jasmine's success with pets included Owain Owen's hob ferret who would no longer go down a rabbit hole, a Great Dane languishing in elegant decline on a chaise longue in a Welsh manor house, and a Siamese cat off its food in Barnswick.

Owain's ferret, she was able to tell him, had developed claustrophobia, which can sometimes be the case with rabbiting ferrets, and consequently was now in retirement. The Great Dane was broody, and if the owner didn't want nature to take its course, something Jasmine herself had always been enthusiastically inclined to do, then she suggested a few soft toys for her to mother. The Barnswick Siamese was simply 'coming it', seeking to be the sole centre of attention. That family, she told the owner, were known for it. She briskly recommended putting its feed out as usual then ignoring it. Something which, it was happily reported later, had been successful. There were times when Jasmine didn't have to make things up.

She had dropped in to give Shelly a lift to Penycwn, to take advantage of a hairdresser salon's weekly offer of a half-price hairdo for the over sixties, something which prompted even Shelly to admit her age.

'I don't know what you want to make a ghost up for. Sounds daft to me,' Jasmine said, sitting down with her coffee, taking her losses out on the others.

'You don't need to pretend to have a ghost,' she went on, scornfully. 'I've told you! You've got a real one. A young servant girl in love with the boot boy or a groom. I've often thought of her since. I hope she was happy. I saw her once, in my mind, standing in the doorway of a cottage, watching her children playing, I think, there was the sound of children playing.'

'Ahh, there's nice,' Annie said, sharing it with Shelly.

'Rhianwen. That was the name that came to me when I saw her, came to me as if she'd told it me, shyly. Rhianwen. Means "fair maiden" in Welsh. I think she was happy,' Jasmine said, after a pause, and sounding doubtful. 'I can bring her back, you know. Come over here with my board and planchette, and—'

'No, no, no, Jasmine,' Humphrey said. 'I read about that stuff the other week. It opens the door, it said, for demonic possession, all that kinda thing.'

'But thank you anyway, darling,' Clem said.

'Oh, sure, Jas, yeah, thank you,' Humphrey said. 'The thing is, Jas, see, with a pretend ghost, you don't get any problems.'

Chapter Sixteen

So far, the fact that Humphrey had promised a sackful of toys he could no longer afford had been his secret, his burden alone to bear. A burden he had decided that must now be shared with the matron, today. Or by the end of the week at the latest. It was the only decent thing to do.

And she would of course have told the ward staff, and they might have told their families, or maybe their friends. But he had to make sure that it didn't go much further than that. What Phineas called 'damage limitation'.

Two days after that, the matron still untold, it was taken out of his hands when he answered the telephone in the hall.

A woman introduced herself as Arabella Beddoes, feature writer for *Marches Life*, a local magazine. She said that they had just done a piece on the Christmas preparations at Kingham General, and the matron had mentioned his super offer of toys for the children's ward.

Humphrey froze. He thought wildly of saying that she had the wrong number, or that Sir Humphrey no longer lived there, or that he had died. Or even that the Matron must have misunderstood.

'Well, yeah, yeah, that's right – er…' was all he said, quietly, glancing towards the kitchen, not knowing if Clem was in there or not.

Arabella took his hesitation for modesty and said that it did him credit, unlike some she could jolly well name, who never gave without wanting to see it in print, and with a photograph of them doing the giving.

'Yeah, well,' Humphrey said modestly, 'you know…'

'But the light from that candle must not be hid, Sir Humphrey,' she went on eagerly. 'There is a wider need, a message if you like at Christmas, for a world in need of it. How far that little candle throws its beam,' she declaimed. 'So shines a good deed in a naughty world.'

Humphrey, busy with his own thoughts, said vaguely that he couldn't agree more. He had to tell her that there had been a mistake. Had to stop it here and now, before it gets into print, with his photograph. And then tell the matron, today, no more putting it off, not now, he told himself, cornered, and saw, not for the first time, her face across the desk that day, the smile that had turned her young again. It would be like telling her that there was no Father Christmas after all.

'It really is the spirit of Christmas at work,' Arabella said breathlessly in his ear. 'And Beverley Kynaston will help spread that message, will help cast that candle beam far and wide!' she added on a high girlish note of excitement.

'Who's Beverley Kynaston?' Humphrey was startled into asking.

'Beverley Kynaston, Sir Humphrey, is a producer at ATV Midlands, one of the companies Daddy's chairman of. They're great chums, so when he was dining with us the other evening, I happened to mention your gift to the sick children, and your arrival in Batch Magna as Father Christmas on a paddle steamer. Everyone at table, including Daddy, thought it was super. And Beverley thought it was *absolutely* super! Loved it. Said it had Christmas written all over it. Said he could see it in one, from Batch Magna to the hospital. A programme simply *begging* to be made. Couldn't be more perfect, unless we had snow. But even Daddy can't arrange that!'

'What programme?' Humphrey asked, while suspecting the worse.

'A television programme,' Arabella said, which is what Humphrey thought it meant. 'How about that, Sir Humphrey! Your good deed in the front rooms of houses across the region. Bevers is already working on a shooting script, and has organised a mock-up from props of a sleigh for you to sit in, driven there, with sleigh bells and fairy lights and carols playing, on the back of a lorry, the route advertised for people to see Father Christmas arriving in town. And Matron will be at the hospital entrance to greet you, with a group of carol singers, the faces of the children in close-up when Father Christmas comes through the ward door bearing his sack of presents, his gift of Christmas. Oh, gosh! It makes one want to believe all over again.'

Humphrey took a deep breath. 'Yes. Yes, right, but, Miss—'

'Arabella, please.'

'Yes, but, Ara—'

'And you needn't think it will stop there!' she assured him, breezy with more good news. 'Bevers is in absolutely *no* doubt that other stations will snap it up.'

'What – across the whole country, d'you mean?' Humphrey said.

'Difficult to believe, isn't it!' she agreed gaily. 'But yes, across the whole country. Your good deed passed on from station to station. Its light a beacon shining from Land's End to John o'Groats. Crikey, it's exciting! Your gift of toys, Sir Humphrey, will have a bit more than the light of a candle shone upon it. And our little magazine will do its bit, contribute our widow's mite. So if you can bear the intrusion, we'd like to visit the boat, if we may, get some background, take a few pics, and all that. Does tomorrow morning suit? We could meet you there. I don't imagine a paddle steamer will be hard to find,' she said cheerily. 'Say ten?'

'Yes—'

'Super! Ciao!'

'Yes, but—' Humphrey said, and heard only the dial tone on the other end.

Then almost dropped the phone when Clem came down the stairs.

He chuckled vaguely and, replacing the receiver, pointed at it. 'A plumber. That was a plumber,' he said, plumbing being on his mind before the phone rang.

'A plumber?' Clem said.

'Yeah, a plumber. Asking if we wanted any plumbing done. Matter of fact we do, I said. In the gatehouse, right? But I told him, I said, unless it's a free offer…' Humphrey chuckled again.

'How very odd,' Clem said, picking up something but not sure what. 'A plumber touting for business in the season of burst pipes.'

'That's what I thought. I thought, hey, wait a minute, it shows this guy can't be any good, right? No thanks, buddy, I told him. Even as a free offer. Who wants the problems afterwards, eh? Any tea on the go?'

Chapter Seventeen

The PS *Batch Castle*, a side-wheeler paddle steamer in the dark gold and Trafalgar blue livery of the old Cluny Steamboat Company, sat on her ropes for winter at the landing stage of the new Cluny Steamboat Company, waiting for flags and bunting, and a steam whistle calling again, a song of summer in Batch Valley.

Once a week in cold weather, Sion, Annie and Owain's son, and the estate's gamekeeper, when gamekeeping was needed, or head gamekeeper, as Humphrey described him, ignoring the fact that the estate only had one of them, would push a hundredweight of coal from John Beecher's yard in the village up the gangway in a wheelbarrow, and into the engine room.

There, her fire was lit to warm her through, and to make steam, to check that the moving parts of her engine still moved as they should, hadn't corroded or seized up.

Tom Parr, a villager who had worked for the old CSC, and did so again as engineer on the summer runs, showed Arabella Beddoes the boat's engine at work when they had steam up, light from the overhead bulkhead lamps travelling up and down on the lovingly polished copper piston rods, the enamel ironwork of the engine a shining post-office red.

'She's getting on now, like me,' Tom told her. 'So in the cold weather we get her joints moving, see, make sure they're all right, like, and blow a bit of steam through her.'

He told her lovingly how it worked, how the boiler turns water to steam, which is fed into pipes, where it expands under pressure to push a piston in the cylinder, which is then passed from the piston to the crankshaft, which turns the paddle wheels.

'Fascinating,' Arabella said politely, her gaze drifting off again to Sion shovelling more coal into the firebox, a young Welsh bullock in a coal-stained singlet, his dark Elvis quiff flattened with sweat.

The photographer snapped Sion at work with his fireman's shovel, and Tom Parr, in engineer's white overalls and the company cap with the gold ribbon from the old CSC before it went bankrupt, and kept in the wardrobe all his redundant years since, a castaway from the River Cluny's past rescued by the new Cluny Steamboat Company.

The Commander was wearing for the visit his shipping master's navy uniform, a white-topped cap with the Strange family coat of arms in a wreath of gold oak leaves, the four gold rings on his sleeves topped with Nelson loops. The photographer took shots of him at the wheel and with Stringbag, officially first mate when underway, with a bunk in the wheelhouse and a ship's ration of dog biscuits.

Arabella, shorthand notebook in hand, wanted the background of the *Batch Castle* and the Cluny Steamboat Company, and Humphrey was happy to tell her.

Happy to be back in that world which his great uncle Cosmo had made, and which he, Humphrey, had brought to life again, breathing steam when the fire of the *Castle* was up, its heat a sun around which everything needed to turn her wheels revolved. Riding her trembling deck with the same sort of pleasure as Sir Cosmo had ridden the decks of paddle steamers on a Victorian Thames, up and down between Greenwich and Hammersmith, finding heaven in a fine drizzle of steamy soot and spray.

And when London County Council had put the entire fleet up for sale after a year of steadily falling receipts, Cosmo had bought four of them, the smallest of the fleet, at a combined price of six thousand pounds. And could only wonder that money, mere money, could buy such things.

Not that Cosmo had any money, or none to spare, and so sold off more of his land, taking another chunk out of the legacy which one day would be Humphrey's.

And if Humphrey had been Sir Cosmo, he would have done precisely the same, inheriting, along with the greatly denuded estate, his love of the music of the wheels, and the sound of a twin-cylinder compound diagonal engine hammering away.

'But how on earth did they get them from London to the river here?' Arabella asked.

And Humphrey told her of their journeying, told her how the small flotilla had sailed downstream to the River Medway and dry dock in Chatham, where they were partially dismantled and hauled over to the railhead on steel rollers for the train to Shrewsbury, pulled there by an engine called *Progress*.

exchange with the public is welcome, even desirable, but only along the lines of, "But enough about me – what did *you* think of my last play or film?"'

'Where do you live then, Rory?' Hazel, back with her white wine again, said. 'If you don't mind me asking.'

'Not at all, Hazel. I live in London. Fulham. I'm here on a visit to my dear and old friend Phineas, who's obligingly showing me the sights I didn't have time to see when here and intent on the next sale, as we salesmen tend to be, as indeed we must be in these competitive times. We're taking the ghost tour when you close.'

'Oh!' Hazel said. 'So am I. I have a free pass. I've worked here for over a year and never done it yet. Mrs Loveridge the landlady is going to cash up and that, and I'm going with a friend, Dora. She's another divorcee,' she added, glancing at Phineas.

'A lot of it about,' Phineas said. 'The tour takes place upstairs, I believe. The two top storeys.'

'Yes, that's right. This place was a hotel until about three years ago, and those two floors have sixteen bedrooms between them, and bathrooms, linen cupboards and that, all empty now. The place changed hands a couple of times since, with nobody doing anything about the empty floors. The present owners, Mr and Mrs Loveridge, haven't been here long, but he's a builder and the plan is to turn the upstairs into bedsits to rent out. We do the tour by candlelight. Spooky! But fun,' she added, looking at Rory.

Chapter Nineteen

Mr Loveridge addressed the fifteen or so people, mostly couples, gathered in the lounge, the biggest of the pub's bars. The landlord had snuff on the lapels of a checked jacket with sagging pockets, a tie with a large horseshoe pin, and a frontage which spoke of his fondness for his own beer, which, as Rory and Phineas had both agreed, was excellent.

The beer pumps were now forbidden, hidden under bar towels at ten thirty each evening, and ten on a Sunday, stilled by the licensing committee in the town hall, the conscience of the town.

The landlord gave the background to the crime as if reading an item in a newspaper in which he had no particular interest, or even confidence that it was true, and then, as if remembering to give them their money's worth, would startle his audience by veering off suddenly and loudly into melodrama.

He told of a Welsh cloth trader in the early nineteenth century, Enoch Morris, a guest at the hotel, who had his throat cut while he slept and robbed of that day's takings.

'The constables were given a name and arrested one Abraham Darby from Birmingham, a saw-pit worker, lodging in the same house as the informant, apprentice bricklayer Joseph Venables. Both young men and both in love with the same girl, Beatrice Hausen, a laundry maid here at the hotel. Darby, Venables said, had confessed to him when drunk. They found a bloodstained shirt in Darby's room, and a gold watch inscribed with the dead man's name. No money was found, and it was never recovered. Young Darby was tried at the Assizes, found guilty and went to the gallows at Shrewsbury Prison, swearing on his mother's life and before God right up until he was dropped, that he was innocent. Joseph Venables left the district soon after, and opened a tripe seller and cheesemonger's shop in Whitchurch. You can draw your own conclusions about that. But it's said that both ghosts, that of the cloth trader and Abraham Darby, roam the rooms upstairs.'

The landlord dug into a waistcoat pocket for a silver-coloured turnip watch on a fob chain hung with charms. Below the waistcoat a few inches of shirt strained at its buttons, his flannel trousers secured like a corset with a wide large-buckled leather belt.

'The tour usually lasts just under an hour. There's no electricity on those floors for safety's sake, because they need rewiring. Not that we'd use it anyway. It's a ghost tour, not the front at Blackpool. We provide candles. And finally, ladies and gentlemen, we ask you to please bear in mind that we can't guarantee ghostly presences. It's not a fix, so we can't lay 'em on to order. They're real – unlike some so-called haunted places,' he finished, leaving Phineas to wonder if he was looking at him.

'In other words, don't ask for your money back,' Dora, Hazel's friend whispered to him. 'Makes me suspicious straight away.'

'Yes,' Phineas said. 'Either that, or the place really is haunted.'

'Ohh, don't say that!' Dora said, and shivered exaggeratedly.

'Well, that's what you paid to see, isn't it?'

'Yes, I know. But... well, you know,' she said and shivered again.

Dora was a few years younger than Hazel, but a tight perm and glasses with lilac-tinted frames made her appear older. She was a civil servant, a librarian, and as Rory had introduced Phineas as a financial consultant, asked him almost immediately at what age he recommended she should take her pension. When she was first allowed to do so at sixty, or wait until official retirement at sixty-five, bearing in mind the cost of living index.

And it is the cost of living index, he told her firmly, that must be borne in mind. The cost of living index, he said again, liking the solid, responsible weight of the words, should and must be at the heart of any decision taken. His advice, as he was sure that all responsible financial consultants would tell her, was to wait and see. To make that decision nearer the first retirement date, when a truer prediction of the cost of living index over the following five years would be available.

And he meant it, too. He thought her a dear little thing, and it was hardly advice that could lead her financially astray. Maybe he was more cut out for this sort of thing than he realised.

He daydreamed sometimes, when on the river, of another life. A financial consultant, maybe, he thought now. In a city somewhere, in a cramped office half-buried in files, many of them work he refused to charge a fee for. A champion of the little man, the small businesses struggling to keep afloat, and the Doras of this world, working tirelessly at all hours, with a secretary who secretly loved him and who made sure he ate at least once a day.

Dora gave him a nudge, and they followed Mr Loveridge up the first flight of narrow stairs, past the living quarters that were once hotel rooms, up another, shorter flight to the second floor, a deal table waiting at the entrance with candles, tin holders and matches on it.

The landlord lit one of the candles using his lighter.

'We don't know which bedroom the Welshman was murdered in, though footsteps heard suggest the top floor,' he said. 'So we'll look at all the rooms, bathrooms included. Although no activity's ever been reported there yet. But we want you to have your money's worth. Keep together please, and if you have to talk, do so quietly. If you hear or see anything, just stand still. People have heard – and seen things,' he said, grinning a Halloween grin at them over the wavering candle flame.

They trooped into the corridor between bedrooms, their candlelight breaking up the darkness, moving it about on walls and ceiling. The air was chilled without the heating on up there, and with a silence that went with it.

Rory was holding his candle holder up above his long black hair, a Cavalier in shadow. Hazel, taking advantage of the situation, slid an arm through his.

'It's like that film I saw—' Dora started.

'Shhh!' Phineas hissed.

'What was that?' one of the men in front said, looking round nervously.

'That was just me going "shhh"!'

'Shhh!' the landlord said.

They made their way slowly along the corridor in the moving dark, keeping together, past the closed doors of what were once bedrooms, behind which anything, or anybody, might wait, their shadows creeping ahead of them.

'What's that?' the landlord said sharply. 'I thought I heard something.'

They came to a halt behind him.

'What's that?' the landlord said again, a few moments later on a louder note, and sounding testy, and somewhere a door slammed. Dora clutched at Phineas's arm.

Rory, let down himself a few times by backstage sound effects coming in late, sympathised. 'Somebody somewhere's not paying attention,' he muttered to Hazel.

'Shhh!' Mr Loveridge said. 'Listen.'

They listened. A woman, walking past the pub, screeched with sudden laughter, the traffic on the street sounding distant.

'Is anybody there?' the landlord said then, as if at a séance, and Dora gripped Phineas's arm again.

'Speak, ghost,' Rory said, an appeal to the fretful shadows of Elsinore Castle, in a low, Royal Academy-trained voice that could have been heard perfectly clearly in the back row of the gallery.

'Drink to me only with thine eyes, so I can keep the bottle,' Phineas sang to Dora.

'Ladies and gentlemen, we must have quiet!' the landlord said.

'Is anybody there?' Mr Loveridge asked again.

'Only us chickens,' some wag said, to stifled giggles.

The giggling stopping abruptly then, when footsteps were heard.

They listened in tense silence to what sounded like pacing, and as if it could be coming from either floor.

'It's like it's coming from up there,' somebody said in a near whisper, glancing up at the ceiling.

'Sounds to me as if it's down here somewhere,' someone else said. 'One of the bedrooms.'

'And it could be either of the two men,' Mr Loveridge said, with grave authority. 'Both for different reasons unable to be at rest in the hereafter. Well, nothing at all happened during the last tour, so maybe this is your lucky night. We'll go to the end of the corridor and then come back and do the bedrooms and the two bathrooms, before going up to the next floor. Come on.'

They came back down the corridor, looking into the rooms, some of them holding back, letting others do the looking.

The bedrooms were bare of even curtains and carpets, their candlelight at home there, in rooms returned to the seventeenth century, gleaming on oak floorboards, on the patina of three hundred years of polish and the sweat of housemaids. The light with which, in one of the rooms, Enoch Morris the cloth trader, with a successful day's business behind him, would have found his way to bed, before waking, briefly, choking bloodily on a nightmare.

A few bedrooms further along, Mr Loveridge opened the door and came to an abrupt halt, the others shunting into him.

He lifted his candle higher, throwing its light on two figures against the wall there. Rory and Hazel, caught in a desperate embrace.

'Come on,' he said, 'we're not licensed for that. Out you go. There's always at least one couple on every tour,' he said. 'Gawd knows why the thoughts of spooks gets them going.'

Rory spread his hands in apology to Phineas. 'I was overwhelmed, dear lad, in the scented dark – she really does wear a most alluring brand – and by her need for a little manly reassurance after hearing a floorboard creak or mice in the wainscoting. What was a chap to do?'

'Do what we came here to do – that's what a chap should do, Rory!' Phineas was able to tell him. 'And I thought I had made what that was perfectly clear.'

'You did indeed.'

'What did you think you were doing, Hazel?' Dora asked indignantly.

'Looking for ghosts,' Hazel said brazenly.

'You may disagree, Rory,' Phineas went on, occupying the moral high ground for once and enjoying the view, 'but I consider that we both have obligations to what amounts to our word.'

'Keep together, please,' Mr Loveridge called back to them, leading the others out of another bedroom.

'Acushla,' Rory said to Phineas, 'I stand chastised, and rightly so. From now on I shall keep my hands, and everything else, to myself. My attention devoted exclusively to the job before us.'

'You want to mind your own business, Dora!' Hazel said, stung into it by the prospect of Rory keeping his hands to himself. 'Come on, Rory,' she said, leading him of by the arm.

'Don't let Norman catch you,' Dora said to her retreating back, but meant more for Phineas's ears.

'Who's Norman?' he asked.

'Her husband,' she said with some satisfaction.

'But they're divorced, aren't they?'

'Oh, she's playing that game again, is she. The last time it was a farmer, a respectable man from Church Pulverbatch. Norman found them in the select bar in the Butcher's Arms. They made a right exhibition of themselves. It was in the *Chronicle*, photographs and all. And of course his wife found out, Well, bound to, wasn't she. Everybody reads the *Chronicle*. Her daughter didn't speak to her for ages over it. And who can blame her. She's a doctor's receptionist and has certain standards to live up to.'

'We're going upstairs now, come along, please,' the landlord said, waving them on, Phineas, with an avid ear for gossip, standing listening to Dora.

'She said she had no children,' he said, walking on with her.

'She's got four!' Dora said, delighted with the lie. 'No children indeed! Typical Hazel, that is. She'd tell you black was white and not blink. Yes, she's my friend. And yes, she has her good points. But telling the truth isn't one of them.'

But Hazel, Dora made clear, had been telling the truth, for once, when she said that she, Dora, was divorced. It was just small things, she said, that had ended the marriage, ten years of small things that in the end became too much.

'The weight of time and small things,' Phineas said, in charge of the candle and leading the way up the narrow staircase, 'is not to be underestimated.'

On the third floor, the traffic below seemed even more remote, a world, the world they knew, away. There was a stronger smell now of candles in the chilled air, the smell of the wax burning down in a darkness that seemed somehow deeper, somehow far less friendly, as if it were the real thing, as if any idea they might have had that the tour was something to laugh at stopped there.

'… And he used to speak with his mouth full when eating, that was another thing,' Dora said confidingly. 'He'd be talking away, usually about football, which was about the only thing he'd get excited about, especially if Shrewsbury Town had won, and I'd see his meal going round, round and round as he talked, like – er…'

'A mixed grill?' Phineas suggested, and Dora laughed.

'Shhh!' Mr Loveridge hissed at them, Rory and Hazel looking back at them suspiciously.

'And if I read something out of the paper to him, something about politics, something like that,' she went on, in a low chatty voice, 'he'd say, "So they say." That's all. "So they say." Never anything else. As if he knew better, or knew something that they or I didn't know. "Never you mind," he used to say, when I asked him what he meant by it. Used to drive me round the bend! Oh, I am enjoying myself,' she said then, putting her arm through his as they walked on. 'But you haven't told me about yourself yet. Are you married, Phineas?'

'Yes,' he said immediately. 'Well, I say yes, but I mean – *almost* married, you know. Almost, but not quite,' he said, not wanting to tell her a total lie.

'You're engaged then,' she said, as if helping him out.

'Well, yes, I suppose I am. Yes,' he said, and chuckled briefly.

'You are funny,' she said, giving him a dig with her elbow.

Only a few of the tour now followed the landlord into the rooms, because they had done all that, or because they were aware that if something more was to happen they were running out of time for it to do so.

The landlord came to a halt and held up a hand. 'Quiet!' he said, and they heard footsteps again, lightly this time, as if creeping stealthily, with intent.

'We've heard that sound before,' he said in a spectral voice, lifting his candle, sending the shadows fleeing. 'It's—' He broke off, frowning at the intrusion of another sort of sound, a knocking sound, a sound that carried urgency in it.

Others heard it, too. 'It's what?' a woman said, an edge of panic in her voice. 'It's what? What is it!'

'What is it – what is it!' somebody else joined in.

'It sounds as if it's up here somewhere,' one of the men said. 'As if someone's trying to get out of somewhere.'

'Or get in,' someone else suggested shakily.

Which is what Norman, Hazel's husband, was trying to do, banging the knocker on the pub door, and determined not to leave until he did.

Thunder turned immediately to wheedling then, when Mrs Loveridge answered. Anything else, he knew, and he wouldn't get over the doorstep.

'I'm sorry, Mrs Loveridge, to disturb you, but I wondered if Hazel was still here. Only she was supposed to going on the ghost tour, and I—'

'Upstairs, Norman,' Mrs Loveridge said, impatient to get back to the television. 'Go on up.'

'Oh, thank you, Mrs Loveridge. That is kind of you. Only I was—'

'The top floors. That's where the tour is.'

Norman thanked her, edging round her with an ingratiating smile, which lasted until he was on the stairs. Then thunder returned.

Mr Loveridge, having worked it out, said, 'It was somebody at the pub door. We get that sometimes, people wanting a drink after hours. Mrs Loveridge would have sent whoever it was on their way with a flea in their ear. But it must have disturbed the atmosphere on the other side, because shortly after those sort of footsteps the scream of the murdered man could usually be heard.'

'How could he scream with his throat cut?' Phineas muttered to Dora. 'Be more like a sort of gurgling sound, I would have thought.'

'Ugh!' she said.

'Awful scream, it was. Awful,' Mr Loveridge said, emphasising it. And a scream followed that seemed to come from the very air, that seemed to feed on itself there, a living thing that was everywhere in the darkness, bloated with dreadful sound.

Two of the women on the tour screamed with it, some of the men half crouching, fearful and alert, as if expecting attack. And the women screamed again then, when Norman burst through the door, the scream dying and the running footsteps which followed drowned by his rage when he saw his wife and Rory standing apart together further down the corridor.

'There she is! There's the trollop! There's the floozy with her fancy man!' he roared.

'Who the devil's that?' Rory said.

'That's Norman,' Dora told Phineas.

'Rory! It's Hazel's husband!' Phineas warned him.

'Norman – get out!' Mr Loveridge said, pointing at the way he'd come in.

'I'll swing for her!' Norman told him. 'I'll kill both of them!'

'Norman!' Hazel said sharply.

'I'll deal with this,' Rory said, slipping out of his sheepskin. 'Women are for weeping.'

'Don't be daft, darlin',' Hazel said, losing the genteel accent she'd affected since meeting him to border Welsh. 'And put your coat on, you'll catch your death.'

'Hello, Norman,' Dora said cheerfully, as Norman went by, intent on his wife and Rory.

And his wife was just as intent on him, her expression as she marched towards him bringing him slowly to a halt.

Mr Loveridge, having witnessed his barmaid dealing with a few unruly customers in the past, folded his arms and waited patiently for her to do the same with Norman, so he could finish up and have his supper.

'It shouldn't take long,' he told the others. 'Apologies for the interruption.'

'How dare you – how dare you!' Hazel snarled at her husband. 'So I'm a trollop, am I? A floozy, is it?'

'Now, Haze,' Norman said, and retreated a few steps.

'She gave him a black eye that time in the Butcher's Arms,' Dora said. 'And hit him with an ashtray. Loves him, see.'

'I see,' Phineas said, not looking as if he did.

'Well, you were flirting with him,' Norman said. 'Will told me, Will Larkin. He saw you from the public bar.'

'I was talking to him. It's my job, boy. The job that helps pay for your beer. Wait till I see Will Larkin.'

'Well, what were you doing together now then? What was that about?'

'We were talking again. Talking. It's what people do. Normal, sociable people, anyway. But then you wouldn't know about that, would you, Norman.'

'Oh, yeah. That's what it's called, is it?' Norman said.

And trying for nonchalance, a man with the upper hand, he leaned casually against a door and immediately disappeared through it into a walk-in linen cupboard, revealing a young man, his mouth dropping open, sitting with a torch and a tape recorder with complicated-looking wires running from it.

Phineas drove back to the Hall to drop off Rory and to pick up Bill Sikes, who'd be sharing the kitchen with the Hall's dogs if the family had gone to bed.

'That Hazel!' Rory said, shaking his head admiringly. 'I had thought that that mixture of gentility and the woman under it would be powerful stuff when uncorked. And have a Welsh accent, as it turns out. I must come here more often.'

'Border accent,' Phineas corrected him. 'Half Welsh, half English. Everything is in halves here. Your final demands and billets doux are either delivered by Post Brenhinol or the Royal Mail. You pay your rates to either a Welsh county council or one on the English side, with the paperwork in both languages. Your telephone operator has either a Welsh or an English accent, and your doctor's practice can be in either country, and your doctors of either nationality. And on Sunday, as you will no doubt discover, when the pubs in bordering Welsh counties are chapel dry still, the Steamer Inn is packed with Welsh speakers calling a truce with the English. We are a backwater, a land half lost and half forgotten between two countries. And happy for it.'

'I'll drink to that,' Rory, Irish and one of life's rebels, said, as the Frogeye, Phineas's canary-yellow Austin Healey Sprite, roared on through the winter countryside, night in the narrow bare lanes falling back in its headlights, the darkness over the fields lit briefly in sweeps by them.

Phineas laughed. 'Poor Norman. And that tape recorder! And the hapless youth caught with his mouth open. That's why of course the door was ajar.'

'And he still missed a couple of cues,' Rory said.

'Well, at least we got our money back.'

'Doing it for charity. Thinks on his feet, that landlord.'

'The story was true,' Phineas said. 'It's the ghosts he made up. And as somebody there said, he could have his collar felt for fraud.'

'He might still have, if the local constabulary get to hear of it.'

'And that, Rory, old man, is what's giving me pause. The ghost of Artemus Strange is a great wheeze and all that, but—'

'But you wouldn't be the one having to answer if questions are asked?'

'Precisely.'

'Yes, that had occurred to me, as well. 'Tis a pity. I liked the idea of a bit of ghostly swordplay.'

'We can of course still go on with the re-enactments. If you're still willing, that is.'

'Of course. What are friends for? Hollywood will just have to be patient. I'll get there. Soon as I've saved up the boat fare.'

Phineas drove on down into Batch Valley, long reading with ease, even at night, the tangled puzzle of lanes that were once drovers' roads, or old cart ways and coffin routes, and crossed a bridge over the Cluny built by monks, and into Batch Magna, his lights burrowing through its lampless High Street, before sweeping up the drive of the Hall.

When he pulled up in the forecourt, Rory, who had been silent for a while, said, 'Phineas, my boy, it occurs to me that there is a way we can produce Artemus, the ghost, without inviting the law to call. If it's done as a piece of theatre. If we call it something else, put it differently. Call it, say, *The Artemus Strange Experience*. Or, better, *The Ghost of Artemus Strange Experience*. Ghosts have pulling power. As Shakespeare knew. And there'd be no risk then of those good people in there being accused of trousering money through false pretences.'

About to get out, Rory then said. 'And – *and*, Phineas, dear chap, if we get hold of a dry-ice machine, for theatrical smoke, you know? If we can borrow or hire one, we can do the swordplay in a sort of ghostly mist. The mist of time. A dance from the past.'

'Rory,' Phineas said, slapping the steering wheel, 'you're a blooming genius.'

Chapter Twenty

The next morning Rory visited Phineas on the *Cluny Belle.*

'Look at the state of this place,' he said, prising Sikes's paws off his chest, the dog's tongue trying to reach his face. 'And I speak as a bachelor, living on his own. Do you ever clean it at all?'

'Of course I do. When needed,' Phineas said, his tone suggesting that it was nowhere near needing it yet. 'Anyway, never mind my domestic arrangements. I rang Maggie an hour ago.'

'Maggie – the one who's the one?'

'Did I say that?'

'You did. If it's same Maggie, the wardrobe mistress at the local rep.'

'Yes, well, anyway. Yes, she's – er – she's the wardrobe mistress at the Kingham Rep. That's right. Maggie. Anyway, I thought I'd ask if there was any chance of us borrowing a dry-ice machine, because the more I think about the idea the more I like it. But they've only got one, and they need that, she said, for the pantomime season coming up.'

'Quite right, too. You simply cannot have a pantomime without dry ice. Be sending fantasy on without its knickers. Does she not know anyone who might—'

'Yes, she gave me a couple of numbers of firms in the Midlands to ring. But their rental machines are out on indefinite hire to restaurants.'

'Ah,' Rory said. 'That gives me an idea. It's certainly worth a try. Can I use your phone? It's a London number.'

'Of course. I'll put the kettle on. We'll have coffee.'

A short while later Rory put down the phone and said, 'We've got one.'

'Great!' Phineas said. 'Where's that – a theatre there?'

'No. A fella in the East End called Eddie Carter. He sells and rents out all sorts of gear, including smoke machines for Halloween parties, nightclub launches, discos, all that sort of thing. He can let us have one, and for as long as we want.'

'How much a week?'

'Nothing. As Eddie said – "I owe you one, son." I haven't seen him for a few years – some of which he could have been banged up as a guest of Her Majesty. But Eddie's old school. A man who pays his debts. Must be getting on now, but in his youth he was very active with a pair of nostrils, as it's called in the trade. A double-barrelled shotgun. Loaded with birdseed and fired at a bank's ceiling it guarantees instant attention, as you can see it would. The business he's got now is maybe a front, to show a bit of legitimate income.'

'Bank ceilings?' Phineas wonderingly,

'He specialised in withdrawals, as he called his bank robberies.' Rory laughed. 'He told me that there's plans to use smoke machines for security purposes, in places like high-class jewellers' shops and banks, installed on the other end of a panic button. "I got out at the right time, Rory," he told me. You know, Phin, I have at times, I must confess, a yen for the outlaw path. The freedom of a life lived entirely on your terms. Taking what you need, when you need it, and be damn to the rules. If, that is, I don't have to shoot anyone, and have a stay-out-of-gaol clause in the contract.'

'Rory, what on earth did you do for this man?'

'I perjured myself on his behalf. I jeopardised my immortal soul and broke the laws of England. I stood in the witness box in the venerable Number One Court at the Old Bailey and swore on the Book that I had seen him at a particular time on a particular day. The particular time and particular day that he was supposed to be bringing down more ceiling plaster in another bank.'

'And you had not?'

'I had not. He told me it was a fit-up by the local CID office, and having heard other accounts of their working methods, I had no trouble believing him. So instead of going down the dock steps, he walked out to a large Bell's in the Magpie and Stump, with the prosecution drowning its sorrows in one bar and a jolly going on in another.'

'And the wages of sin is a dry-ice machine. Where do we pick it up?'

'At his place in Spitalfields. He rents a place in one of the lanes off the market there. But the size of the machine may be a problem. It's a big bulky old thing, by the sound of it. We could always tie it, I suppose to—'

'We'll take Henrietta, the Hall's shooting brake. Plenty of room in her.'

'I'll put up the petrol money.'

'Rory, you're a sportsman, but there may be no need. Or need only for a top-up. They keep her tank full in case of a sudden windfall of paying guests arriving at Church Myddle station, or Shrewsbury, as sometime happens. And when we get going they'll have something coming in again. It's all turning out rather well.'

Leaving Bill Sikes in the company of the Jack Russell, Tip, and Henry the lurcher, they left the Hall the following morning, a Friday, in the shooting brake, and pointed her nose in the general direction of London.

They had made good time and stopped for lunch in Oxford, at a pub Phineas knew from his university career.

'A career rather on the short side, as it turned out,' Phineas said.

'They fired you,' Rory said.

'"Rusticated" is the term Oxford and I prefer. Has its roots in Latin. Rustication, of or in the countryside. The rusticated student being sent back to his or her family in the country. I had a family living in the country then, but they didn't want me either. Which is why I was at Oxford in the first place, as I tried to explain to the Dean, or anybody else who would listen.'

'Ah, well, never mind. I'll buy lunch. I never heard, incidentally,' Rory went on, when they ran into a bit of traffic in the middle of the town, 'why you *were* rusticated. Such a pretty word. Like something that should be crowned with a circlet of summer flowers, accompanied by villagers tripping an ancient measure and the tinkling of folk bells.'

'It arrives in the post, in cold print. I'd like to claim some picaresque reason, something that had dash and drama to it, such as Richard Burton the explorer challenging someone to a duel, or the poet Landor trying to shoot a fellow student who kept him awake at nights. But there wasn't even a girl involved. I simply failed all my prelim exams,' he confessed. 'And after that didn't bother to turn up at all. I mean, what was the *point*, I asked myself?'

'"I simply failed my prelim exams",' Rory echoed. 'I put it to you, Mr Cook, that you failed those exams because you didn't work hard enough,' he said, the junior prosecution barrister he'd played in the stage play of *Hostile Witness*.

'Well, I – er—'

'Is that, or is that not, the case?' he demanded.

'Well, I suppose you might—'

'And I put further it to you, that the reason you didn't work hard enough was women and song. Not to mention drink.'

'Well, it's true I—'

'Is that not the case!'

'Well, yes, but—'

'That'll be all, Mr Cook, thank you. No further questions, m'lud.'

The traffic moved on into St Giles' Street, where they found a parking space, and walked up to The Eagle and Child pub.

'Or The Bird and Baby, as some wag named it,' Phineas said, entering it, a place of alcoves and small narrow rooms, with a cautious sort of air, as if his past might be waiting for him, a reproach for the failed prelim exams, for his drinking, and his careless way with the women he had known.

They sat with plates of freshly baked mixed game pies with mashed potatoes and Savoy cabbage under a portrait of a benign-looking J.R.R. Tolkien tweedily smoking a pipe, an author who, with others such as C.S. Lewis, had added their names to the long history of the pub.

When they were sitting back afterwards with cigarettes and the clean pale gold of two well-kept pints of bitter, Rory commented on the odd name.

'Well, my memory's a bit shaky,' Phineas said, 'but it's either to do with the Earl of Derby and a high-born baby found in an eagle's nest. Or, more obscurely, the emperor Hadrian and his beautiful boy lover Antinous, who drowned. Shortly before that happened, Hadrian had been warned by an oracle that only the sacrifice of a person much loved by him would save him from some great danger about to befall him. So was the young Antinous pushed, or did he fall? You must, as the landlord of the Blue Boar would say, draw your own conclusions. Happy days, old thing,' he added, lifting his pint.

'He named stars after Antinous,' Phineas said on their way out. 'A constellation. Writ his name in the heavens.'

Chapter Twenty-One

It was late afternoon, the light hardening, when the shooting brake turned in to Spitalfields in London's East End.

Outside a lorry compound, a fire from the night burned on, fed by wood from broken crates and fruit boxes, potatoes and other scavenged leavings from the streets round the fruit and vegetable market, baking slowly in the piled whitewash of ash.

The men gathered to its heat, sitting around it, or dozing, were figures left behind from the night. Scarecrow figures tied with string, bulky with odds and ends of other clothes under their topcoats, as if stuffed with straw, their ravaged faces and hair wild with dirt caught in the glare of daylight, some of them shouting at the world, at life, as it went by.

'I've never known that fire be out,' Rory said as they drove past them. 'And the poor sods certainly need it in this weather.'

'One of them was killed there a couple of years ago, I remember reading.'

'I didn't know that!'

'Yes. And in a particularly horrid way, too. That was in the winter. It was snowing, and the poor fellow fell asleep where he stood. Drunk, maybe. But where he stood was in front of the entrance of that lorry compound, his body part-hidden apparently by snow and right in the path of an articulated lorry reversing out.'

'Jesus!' Rory said.

'And one can only imagine the state of the driver when he found what he'd driven over.'

They passed the market pub, The Gun, with a nod to a shared past, to memories of Chelsea parties, or what was left of them, ending up there among the market porters at six in the morning.

'I've been back there a few times since,' Rory said. 'For the odd morning livener. Good people,' he added, meaning the East End open-hearted warmth of the family that ran it.

A few minutes later they drove down a lane of rag-trade sweatshops, and under an arch of dirty yellow London brick, its walls littered with fly-posters and the remains of old ones, a local history of shop sales, rock bands, exhibitions, boxing matches, concerts, eating places and warnings of Armageddon.

Eddie's business sat between one repairing market barrows and a second-hand furniture warehouse. They turned in through open wooden gates topped with iron spikes, into a yard with cobbles of the sort that Jack the Ripper had stalked in the night-time rookeries of a Victorian Spitalfields.

'Jack at work in a London fog,' Phineas said, getting out.

the gates, referring to a Soho club he used to frequent, and making a sideward slashing movement with the edge of his left hand, as if he were still one of the chaps, as if he still had a diamond ring on its pinkie, standing there still after they had disappeared.

Chapter Twenty-Two

They decided on Club Arana, in a building which, like many in Soho, was early seventeenth refaced with a Georgian facade. The blue door and its stained-glass fanlight were badly in need of a wash. The narrow staircase with a slight tilt to it and a threadbare carpet, running up from a hall and living quarters, had a furtive, red-light air to it, and carried a faint lingering smell of disinfectant and stale drink.

The club, one room on the first floor, had a ceiling decorated with fishing nets and plastic floats, the furniture wicker chairs and glass-topped tables, and a bar with bamboo uprights and veneer under a roof of synthetic straw.

The club owner Maurice had borrowed money to re-style it that way, and renamed it to please a young Polynesian lover, calling it by his name. Arana, he'd say, means 'handsome' in Polynesian, nodding at the proof of it in a large framed holiday photograph under the optics. Arana, lazily sure of his looks, offering them up with a bored half smile while sitting on the side of a swimming pool, as if not wasting any more than that on whoever was holding the camera.

Not long after that he had gone off with someone else, leaving Maurice in debt and with no money to strip out the memories. Memories in the fake palm fronds that were wilting now, the netting on the ceiling sagging in parts, and the odd bit of plastic falling from the synthetic straw roof.

The place was almost empty. A large Greek doorman drinking retsina at the bar, a couple of girls with chunky Samsonite make-up cases stopping off between strip clubs. A few runners from the film company offices in Wardour Street, with metal film canisters, their badges of office, drinking beer from bottles and gossiping around a table.

A skinhead, perched on a stool one end of the bar in a bomber jacket and Doc Marten boots, glanced round at them when they laughed, as if hoping it might be at him.

Maurice, who called himself mother, and who had a motherly heart that life had finally taught him to keep at bay, giving him a new expression to go with it, one of cautious severity, had long finished with tears over Arana. Although there were times, when his thoughts were elsewhere, when he seemed open to being less cautious, and when those tears seemed much more recently finished with.

But he no longer wore the Polynesian shirts and the seashell and shark teeth necklaces as he did when his future had two in it and a planned beach bar on Arana's home island. He was dressed in black dress trousers and pleated white shirt and black dickie bow, like the Ritz and Savoy cocktail barman he once was, his head, bald like a monk with a fringe of greying hair, polished by the coloured fish-float lights up under the synthetic thatched roof of his bar.

'Oh, look!' he greeted them when they walked in. 'The terrible twins. Didn't I bar you two when you were last here?'

'No,' Phineas said. 'That was some other place, Maurice.'

'Thank gawd for that,' Maurice said, producing the members' book. 'I need the money.'

'Yes, where are the people?' Rory asked.

'It's early yet, my dear, these days,' Maurice said, glancing up at a wall clock in the shape of a ship's wheel. 'Since the Jug and Bottle round the corner acquired new owners their morning sessions seem to get longer every day, taking money from customers which before that would have gone over the bar here by now. Makes you wonder who they're paying off in West End Central, doesn't it,' he said, and, clamping a hand to his mouth, took it away only to add, 'Not another word from me! I've said too much already. What can I do you for?'

Just under an hour later, Maurice was briskly and happily serving customers finally locked out of the Jug and Bottle. Phineas was standing at one end of the bar, listening with an intelligent, thoughtful air to a young female artist in a yellow Peace & Love paint-stained T-shirt and tight jeans, talking about the New Expressionism, how she was getting more of who she was, her inner self, on canvas by painting with her eyes closed.

While at the other end of the bar Rory was talking to the skinhead, Les.

Les had a swastika tattooed on his forehead and a line round his neck with the caption, 'Cut Here'.

'People,' Les was arguing with vague force, stabbing a finger in the direction of the street, 'ought to go back from where they bleeding well come from!'

'Where would that be now?' Rory enquired with interest.

'Well, I don't bleeding well know, do I! Where they come from. And the Irish,' he added, readying himself for an answer, shifting his position on the stool, his fists curled and waiting on the bar.

'What!' Rory said. 'And would you have removed from the hospitals of this country the ministering hands of countless angels?'

'Eh?'

'Nurses, dear,' Maurice told Les, passing with a customer's drink from the optics.

'And who, Les, would make the roads, the motorways, dig clay for the sewer trenches? Who would build those eyesores that blight our cities, those monuments to civic egos and vulgar imagination, and then charge us for the treat on the rates? Answer me that now.'

Les stared at him, thrown off balance, and not altogether understanding the question, never mind having an answer. He looked away with a sneer, as if that were his answer, to a man who hid behind words.

And, digging into his pockets for money, found he didn't have enough for another pint.

''ere, Maurice,' he said, 'Can you let me have a bit of whatsit – you know, just till I pick up me giro?'

Maurice looked sadly amused. 'Don't be silly, dear. God didn't give much in the looks department, but she did make sure, bless her, that I knew enough not to start giving away my stock.'

'You wouldn't be giving it away! As I said, it's just—'

'I'll get it, Maurice,' Rory said. 'With another round.

And one yourself while you're at it. Phineas!' he called down the bar. 'Don't be wasting the club's time, see that off.'

Les watched Maurice serving the drinks with a slight frown, as if it were something else he didn't understand.

And then picking up something he did understand, the pint of lager Maurice had put in front of him, looked from it to Rory and grinned.

'Yeah, well. Thanks. Thanks, Rory. Cheers, mate!'

'Slainte!' Rory said.

''ere,' Les said then, confidingly, 'and you were right, about nurses, being angels and that. My mum's one.'

'Ah, Irish, is she?'

'Irish? Nah, she's from Hackney, born and bred. No, I meant she's a nurse.'

'Phin, this is Les,' Rory said then, Phineas joining them after the artist had left to find more of herself on canvas.

'His mother's a nurse. Phin likes nurses. Been out with lots of them.'

'Almost married a couple of them,' Phineas added. 'You married, Les?'

'Nah.'

'Well, if ever you get round to it make sure it's a nurse.'

'Well, if she's anything like my mum I will.'

'Who was the woman?' Rory asked.

'That was Tabs. Tabitha to you. She's an artist with a studio in Poland Street. Her new thing is – er – New Expressionism. Fascinating. She—'

'What happened to the old Expressionism?'

'Art, Rory, particularly modern art,' Phineas said, with the suggestion of a quote coming up, 'must not – should not, stand still. It should constantly seek the truth of who we are.'

'And who we are, according to some modern art I've seen, is very odd indeed.'

Phineas ignored him and addressed himself to Les. 'It's a search, Les, for externalising inner truth.'

'I get ya, Phin,' Les said obligingly, with the prospect of another free pint in the offering.

'The subjective,' Phineas said, remembering another bit of it, 'made objective. And to ensure there's as little as possible blocking, or interfering, with the communication from the inner to the outer she does it with her eyes closed.'

'Does what with her eyes closed?' Rory asked, switching his attention from a couple who had just entered, the female in brown suede boots and showing an enticing flash of miniskirted legs under a long black overcoat.

'Paints, Rory, paints. Don't be obtuse,' he said, and indicated to Maurice that he wanted to buy a round.

'All art, you see, Les,' Phineas went on, having bought his attention with a fresh pint of lager, 'is basically self-expression.'

'Yeah, I see, Phin.'

'So New Expressionism is – er... is new self-expression. Only more so. Right?'

'Yeah, right.'

'Gets straight to it, Les, see. Cuts out as it were the middle man. Basically,' he added.

And not long after that glanced at his watch, and then at the ship's wheel on the wall.

'Rory, have you seen the time?' he said accusingly.

Rory looked at the wall clock and then at his watch. 'That's the right time sure enough.'

'We'll never get there before Eddie locks up now.'

'Yes, well, Phineas, it's probably just as well, you know. Considering what we've had to drink. And we'd have to navigate the rush hour traffic out of London. A situation in which surely disaster lurks. I'll give him a ring. Tell him we'll pick the brake up tomorrow. That's the best thing. We can crash at my pad tonight. Far more sensible. Then we'll move on. Must be a bit more life than this about.'

'Far more sensible,' Phineas agreed, with a sensible sort of air. 'And when you've finished with the phone, I'll ring the Hall, put them in the picture as well,' he said, referring to the payphone on the stairs landing, and feeling even more sensible about things.

'Phin,' Les said, when Rory had gone, 'you and Rory can crash at our place tonight if you like, out in Hackney. Seeing as you like nurses, like. My mum's off till tomorrow. Be no problem. She's not like me, you know. She's very refined, my mum. And pretty, too. And only about your age.' He regarded Phineas solemnly.

'Well, that's very decent of you, Les, but we've got things to do, you know, people to see. And we're behind as it is. Besides, I don't think your dad would approve.'

'Him? He buggered off ages ago. But I wouldn't mind if he did turn up again, so I could give him a good kicking for the way he treated my mum. The bastard!'

Les looked suddenly much younger, his face clenched and as if near to tears at something he still didn't fully understand.

And Phineas hesitated. He considered for a moment taking up the invitation. That moment where the romantic lived, in a world where anything might happen, and often should. A world where most people saw only windmills. A moment that in the past had ended in three failed marriages, and several near misses, as he afterwards realised, when back in the world most people lived in.

And he considered doing it again, now. Considered travelling to Hackney, tonight, and wooing Les's mum the nurse, to make up for things in her life, wooing her with tenderness and gratitude for the gift Les had offered him. Saw her quite clearly blooming again in its light, saw her as wife number four and Les as his stepson, saw perfectly the complete and happy world they had made for themselves there.

'Look – look, Les,' he said almost guiltily, as if he too were also deserting him, also buggering off. 'Look, we'll have to go when I've made my phone call, but...' And unable to find anything else to say, furtively took a fiver from his post-office money and shoved it into a pocket of Les's bomber jacket. 'Have a drink on me.'

He could always, he told himself, borrow another one off Rory.

Chapter Twenty-Three

Phineas came away from his phone call to the Hall looking thoughtful. They need, he told Rory, out on the street, Henrietta without fail tomorrow morning. They've got a weekend booking for a family of four, arriving at Shrewsbury.

'They would have, wouldn't they,' he added, as if it showed a complete lack of consideration.

'What time tomorrow?'

'Well, I suppose it could be worse. The train gets in at twelve.'

'Eddie opens up at eight. At least he does on a weekday. If he does so tomorrow we should be able to make it. The London traffic on a Saturday doesn't pick up usually till later on in the morning.'

'Well, we had better check that he does open up at eight.'

'Yeah, right, I'll give him another ring,' Rory said, not moving, both undecided where to have the next drink.

The sun had set on London, the lights and the neon that belonged to the Soho night gathering in the dusk, turning the figures on the street into shadows. On the other side across from them, above the recessed door of a surgical appliances shop, the shape of a small Christmas tree was picked out in flashing fairy lights, bright splashes of colour against the soiled London brick, backlit panels across the top of the plate glass of the shop advertised NHS trusses, elastic hosiery and abdominal supports.

Phineas nodded at it. 'Your old job.'

'It's where I got the idea from. I went out with the daughter once. She left me for one of their customers. Said he needed her more than I did. I didn't ask for details.' Rory shook his head. 'Hazel – what a woman,' he said wistfully, nostalgic for what he had missed, rather than known.

'Wonder if she's still beating Norman up?' Phineas said.

'A barmaid's right-hander. Well, we can't stand here all night. Where to, then?'

'Muriel's?' Phineas suggested.

'Or the Iron Lung… No, wait! I've got it,' Rory said. 'The Rehearsal Club. Joanna and her mate are always in there. And I can use the use the phone.'

'Who's Joanna and—'

'They flog perfume in Swan and Edgar's.'

'What's her mate's name?'

'Tina. She's a blonde. At least she was the last time I saw her.'

'Mmm. That would round our little London trip off nicely.'

'Precisely what I was thinking. A taxi for four to Fulham with supplies.' Rory looked at his watch. 'The shop closes at six, I think, but by the time we've got there and had a couple of drinks. And they're worth waiting for.'

'Lead on,' Phineas said, the day looking suddenly promising.

The Rehearsal Club was just off Shaftsbury Avenue, the lights from there putting that part of the street in half shadow. It was in a basement, its window overlooking an area with crates of empties and a couple of dustbins in it, the panes dressed with small drifts of spray-on snow, and a shiny red 'Merry Xmas' sign.

On their way down to it the sound of a piano rose to meet them.

'That's more like it!' Phineas said.

He changed his mind when they went in. The room under its bright festive decorations looked as if it were waiting for a party that hadn't bothered to turn up. There were only four people in it, which included the pianist and the middle-aged woman in a smart suit who managed it, reading the *Evening Standard* behind the bar.

The two customers were sitting at the bar counter, a young man, head lowered over his arms, as if drunk, or crying, and a girl talking to him, an arm round his shoulders.

'Strewth!' Phineas said. 'Even Maurice's place was livelier than this.'

Rory was looking at the pianist. 'Good God,' he said, 'it's Claude Somerville. I thought he was dead, the dear old love.'

'Rory!' the girl at the bar cried, and rushed to him in a small performance of greeting, hugging him, and then dragging him into the centre of the room under a sprig of mistletoe.

'You are naughty,' she pouted at him after the festive kiss.

'Why's that now?' he said, trying to remember behind his smile.

'You said you'd ring.'

'Ah, yes, sure, I remember now. A dark time for me, it was. I had to go home. Somebody sick. Awful sick. Touch and go for a while, doctors shaking their heads and a priest at the ready. It had to be bad for me to forget you.'

'Listen to him!' she said to Phineas, running her eyes over him.

'Phineas, Eve,' Rory said, introducing them. 'Eve is not only beautiful but an actress of rare talent.' He nodded at the man at the bar. 'And who's yer man?'

'Soon,' she said earnestly, 'you will not need to ask. That is Vladislav Mikhailov. A major, major playwright, explores all the great themes of the human condition. Love, war, death, political strife. There's a bombing and two assassinations in the first act of his current work alone. But he's before his time. Theatres in this country are run by businessmen, philistines, counters of seats.'

'Had a knockback?' Rory suggested.

'Yes, poor baby. Absolutely wounded by it. I must get back to him!' she said, as if in earnest appeal at Rory urging her to stay, torn between the two men.

Rory signed them in and bought drinks, including one for the pianist, and took it over to him.

Back at the bar he said, 'If you had been on the Avenue in the twenties and thirties, Phineas, you'd have been blinded by Claude's fame. Spelt out in large megawatts wherever musical theatre was playing. His face daily in the society columns, and on film posters.'

'I thought the name was familiar,' Phineas said.

Claude paused between numbers, and Rory raised his glass, returning his salute for the gin he'd just bought him.

The pianist was wearing stained and creased flannel trousers, patent leather dress shoes cracked with wear, and a dinner jacket from another age, with a dusting of cigarette ash on the wide, pointed silk lapels. Hair that had once been black and slick with Brilliantine was now white, a carefully arranged bouffant, a last stand against age, tinged with yellow and sitting on his head as light as smoke.

Rory asked to use the phone, and after listening to the engaged tone at Eddie Carter's end, put it down and said to Phineas, 'I bet it's Rita. She was a listening ear for the wives and girlfriends of East End villains all those years, when their men had run into the law. And she's still listening now, he tells me, running a sort of helpline. They didn't all retire with Eddie.'

He asked the woman behind the bar, who managed the place for the people who owned it, and a couple more drinking clubs in Soho, if Joanna and Tina, the girls from Swan and Edgar, still came in. She said they did, but as it was Friday evening and late closing, didn't expect them until after seven.

With over an hour to wait, they decided that they had to see somebody first. They told her that they'd be back at seven, if the girls should come in before then.

Claude returned Rory's wave of goodbye as they left, his voice lifted in an Al Bowlly number. A flamboyant, practised wave, as if acknowledging far more than that, as if acknowledging perhaps the adoration of the world he had once lived in. A world he half lived in still, whether performing or not, with the collusion of gin and the lights at night on the Avenue.

Out on the street again, Phineas said, 'Any longer in there and I'd have been sobbing with the Russian.'

'Never mind, with luck we've got the girls to look forward to. Well, the pubs are open. Where to?'

'The French?' Phineas suggested. 'Say hello to Gaston.'

'Yeah. Yeah, the French. But let's have a quick one in the Weighed Off first, as we're down this way. For Eddie. And I can try the phone again.'

'Good idea. We owe him that.'

'He'll appreciate it,' Rory said, on their way there. 'Like a lot of old-school villains, he's a sentimentalist. Rita, his wife, is a jewel. She's always been there for him, and if all he brings home these days are his bunions then she won't complain. She's made a good life for them both, and it stands out a mile that Eddie wouldn't have it any other way. But it's also obvious that part of him misses the other life sometimes, misses the chaps.'

'Weighed off' was underworld slang for a court sentence, something which the club's founder, now dead, of natural causes, had been on the receiving end of several times in his career.

The last time he went up the steps to the dock of the Old Bailey, to hear the finding of the jury back in the early 1950s, he, like Eddie Carter, had walked free. And with the proceeds of the robbery he'd been found innocent of, and a sense of the ironic, had opened the club and retired from a life of crime.

Many of the club's members were still busy in that life, a membership which included musicians, artists, barristers, judges, actors, prostitutes, MPs, writers, silks, stage door keepers and pornographers, policemen, both off duty and undercover, and the odd dissolute peer of the realm.

The front door of the club was up a short flight of worn stone steps between elegant black and gold painted railings.

The club was a much bigger affair than the Arana or the Rehearsal, with a large bar on the ground floor and a billiards room and dining room one floor up. Once the Victorian townhouse of a wine merchant, it was in use as a dressmaking factory before being turned into a club, and its cellars once again used for what they were intended for, the better vintages opened upstairs in the members' dining room.

The reception desk in a corridor on the ground floor was the domain of Fay, a grandmother several times over, who read her library books behind it and got on with her knitting, a cottage industry of woollen things for her growing army of family.

She put aside a bit of intricate work on the toe of a pink bootee to produce the members' signing-in book. In the bar a few yards from her, some of the most feared men in London were drinking and chatting. The Weighed Off, its street door kept open in warm weather, was not a club that needed a bouncer.

Rory came back from phoning Eddie on the payphone near Fay's desk, and picked up the drink Phineas had waiting for him.

'Any luck?' Phineas said.

'Yes,' Eddie answered. 'It was the two of them taking turns on the phone, but nothing to do with villains. Their daughter's having a baby. They're going to be grandparents.'

'Ah,' Phineas said, and smiled vaguely at the news.

'Anyway, tomorrow's no problem. He starts at eight every Saturday. He'll have the gates open and waiting for us.'

'Good old Eddie.'

'He said as we're here to ask for somebody called Frankie Mitcham. To give his best to him. They were close mates apparently, did time together. And if Mr Mitcham isn't here, the message will get passed on.'

'"The message will get passed on." Why do I hear sinister intent in that? Must be this place, looking at some of them here,' Phineas said, meaning a group of men sharing a corner of the carved mahogany bar.

They were the school bullies grown up, expensively barbered and tailored, their long-collared shirts open to a show of chest hair and the gold of a medallion, their wrists and fingers heavy with more gold. They were the ones who never entirely managed to hide who they were under the money, who couldn't *help* who they were. Who, when dining upstairs, aired knowledge gained through wine appreciation courses in a manner that not only defensively challenged the wine waiter, but also intimidated certain other diners, the very company they were keen to impress.

Rory asked the barman if Frankie Mitcham was in the club. The barman couldn't see him there and didn't think he'd been in for a while. He suggested that they ask the group at the bar.

A silence fell when Rory said he was looking for Frankie Mitcham, the faces turned towards them expressionless.

Then one of them asked who they were. He did so without seeming to move his lips, his short, wide neck disappearing into a rather pretty floral shirt with matching tie, his eyes as small and as hard as pebbles.

Rory said they were friends of Eddie Carter, and when Eddie knew they were dropping in there for a drink he'd asked them to give Frankie Mitcham his best.

'He and Rita are going to be grandparents, he's just told me on the phone,' he added, for want of something else to say in the face of their unblinking, silent attention. 'Their daughter, Rose.'

One of them nodded. 'That's right, Rose.'

'In Harlow,' Rory said, thinking something else was called for. 'Runs a pet shop there with her husband Terry.'

There was a brief silence, and then somebody broke it.

'Well, I think I speak for the rest of the chaps here when I say that when you next talk to Eddie, son, give him and Rita our heartiest congratulations,' he said, to a chorus of agreement.

Then somebody else put in, 'Frankie's wintering, as it happens, in his villa on the Costa del Sol. Needs a bit of sun on his bones now he's getting on. Just don't tell him I said that,' he added with a chuckle, a chuckle that said something extra about Frankie Mitcham, whether he was getting on a bit or not.

'I know you,' one of the men, who'd been staring at Rory, said then. 'I've just placed you. You were up the steps for a blag involving a shooter at the Bailey a couple of years back. Am I right? I was there as a character witness for Danny Fyle,' he told the others.

'Even the Archbishop of Canterbury giving witness couldn't have helped Danny,' somebody else said. 'The boy was due, so down he went.'

'Am I right?' the man said again to Rory. 'No need to be shy in this company, son.'

'You've got a good memory,' Rory said, having realised that the dock he was referring to must have been the one on a television screen, when around that time he'd played an armed robber in *Crown Court*.

'What way up did that land?' the man asked.

And that was Rory's cue, that was the time for him to explain what sort of dock he had been in, to thank the man for watching and say he hoped he liked the show.

But the actor got there first, the actor and something in him that was drawn to risk. 'I was in the Magpie and Stump not long after that, with a large Bells in me hand. The jury, God bless 'em, saw through the lies told, the officers of the law who perjured themselves in the name of ambition and a bent collar,' Phineas heard him say, his accent more Dublin than Galway.

Heard him and laughed, as if at a not particularly good joke, and was about to indicate that that was what it was, a joke, when Rory went on,

'It was a fit-up by the Dublin Garda. A certain DCI, God rot him, who's been trying for years to tuck me away. A man who has contacts in your Scotland Yard, and knew, through a dirty little grass, a gobshite from the north side, that I was in London when the robbery went down. I'm sure I don't need to fill any more of it in.'

177

'No, you don't, son,' the man with the matching floral shirt and tie said, stirred into speech at the mention of a grass. 'Do you know who the dirty toerag is?'

'Indeed I do. He's not the only informant in Dublin. It's the reason, gentlemen, I'm back in the Smoke. The little gurrier, hardly out of the slums before, he's here as a tourist, polluting the air in your fair city. And I know where he's holed up. I've followed him a couple of times, when he's been out sightseeing. Took a pot shot at him the other day, strolling across Hampstead Heath with his little camera, but I had the distance wrong. I will not miss the next time. Yer man will not be going home this side of the stars,' he added, starting to enjoy the role.

'I'm Sean, by the way, Sean Kelly. And this is Clive Bellamy-Sinclair,' he went on, introducing Phineas. 'Clive has a tongue on him like silver, polished by Eton and Oxford, and a career in the diplomatic service. A career which ended abruptly when, as Third Secretary in Abu Dhabi, it was discovered that he was taking deposits on London pied-à-terres, apartments seeped in the grandeur of Empire in Horse Guards, overlooking the green of St James's Park and handy for trooping the colour, Coutts bank, and Harrods.'

'Nice one, son,' somebody said, among mutterings of approval.

'This man, gentlemen,' Rory went on, encouraged, 'armed with nothing but his accent and a clipboard, once came within a signature on a chequebook to selling Anne Hathaway's cottage in Stratford to a Japanese billionaire anglophile. With the assurance that is the Old Etonians' by right, he claimed that a plastic, much lighter replica, the product of the latest technological advance in the use of the material in housing, was going to be erected in its place, because of serious wear and tear and creeping subsidence.'

'Blimey!' somebody said.

'Yes. And he almost brought it home, too. Yer man had his chequebook out, and Clive was lending him a Biro, when didn't the Japanese's wife turn up, dripping diamonds and haute couture, and demanded in that boorish way some of the rich feel that they're entitled to, that he furnish proof of who he said he was.'

'Oops?' one of the men, in a silk suit and the air of a successful businessman, suggested.

'"Oops" is right, sir,' Rory said. 'Under the covering fire of indignation that his word as a gentleman was being questioned in that vulgar manner, he had to retire sharpish. Clive is not given to detail and planning, gentlemen. His is the temperament of the moment, the art wrought when the iron is hot, the instinct and spontaneity of the true artist.'

'Still – *lovely* stroke,' another man said, shaking his head admiringly at Phineas. Phineas lifted a modest hand in acknowledgement and smiled on as if he'd forgotten it was there.

'I've always appreciated our white-collar colleagues,' somebody else said, and showed it by going into a boxer's crouch and mock punching Phineas. 'Every time a bit of graft like that makes the linens, even if he did come away with no wages, it reminds the public that we're not all blunt instruments and a pair of nostrils. With respect to your bit of necessary biz across the river, Phil,' he added to the man with the short neck.

Phil accepted it, nodding and grunting something.

'There's a talent and front going untapped there,' the man in the silk suit said, eyeing up Phineas. 'He just needs the right sort of partner. And a good suit. Have a drink, lads,' he added, putting a hand in the air for the barman without looking for him first, a hand that expected to be obeyed, while smiling at Phineas, his eyes like teeth.

Phineas took a hurried glance at his watch, a man who had just realised the time, and was about to say something about them being expected elsewhere and late, when he saw what he first thought must be some sort of fancy dress lark – the sudden appearance of a large uniformed constable bobbing about under his helmet, followed immediately by more of them, all built for trouble.

And then a man who wasn't in uniform, and didn't need one, held up a sheet of paper and assured the room that they did have a warrant.

He introduced himself as Detective Inspector Rawlings, based at West End Centre police station, and, aware that he might be addressing the odd MP or Queen's Counsel, or even an assistant commissioner from the Yard, among the members present, apologised politely for the intrusion, and went on, 'We won't keep you long. We'll try not to inconvenience anyone, but I'm afraid that I must insist that no one leaves the premises until we've finished. I'm sure you'll understand. Thank you,' he added, and, looking about seemingly casually, glanced over at the group at the bar.

One of the men there, standing at the back of the group, discreetly pointed at Phil, the big man with the floral matching shirt and tie.

'Off you go,' the inspector said, pointing two constables in his direction, and more of them moved in with handcuffs then, when the man next indicated Phineas and Rory.

Chapter Twenty-Four

Phineas sat in a cell in West End Central police station in a state of disbelief – or rather that state of disbelief theatre audiences are asked to leave behind when they take their seats. He at once believed and did not believe in the situation they were in. But unlike a theatre audience neither he nor Rory could get up and leave.

He just hoped that the whole thing would be cleared up in time to get the shooting brake back to meet the Shrewsbury train at midday tomorrow.

But that hope, when he remembered, kept remembering, in that state of suspended disbelief, the reasons for their detainment, put to them and typed up in the CID office, then given again by the arresting officer, Inspector Rawlings, to the custody sergeant, was a small, frail thing beating against the official words and the stone of his cell.

He had been arrested on suspicion of a serious fraud, with rather serious remarks in his copy of the arrest paper. Unnerving remarks about misrepresenting himself as a local government official, and the attempted sale of public property, emphasising, in the interests of strengthening a police case, that the said property, with its historical association, was central to the economic and cultural worth of the town of Stratford-upon-Avon, and beyond that should be regarded as part of the nation's heritage.

Serious, grown-up words, words which carried in them the solemn, full-wigged weight of the law.

While Rory, occupying a cell further along, was being held on suspicion of attempted murder.

On the walls of Phineas's cell, among the crude artwork, mad scribblings, the bald head and long nose of Kilroy peering over yet another wall, and a request to help the hard-working officers of this police station by beating yourself up, was the message, scored in large, angry-looking capitals into the green institutional paintwork, that Benji Taylor-Watkins was innocent.

Phineas told him that he knew how he had felt. Were he to ever get out, and kill Rory, it surely would be justifiable homicide.

He had left it too late to tell people it was a joke, just Rory having a stupid joke. He'd said it as they'd bundled them, handcuffed, out of the club, Fay showing little interest in the result of the raid, still knitting away behind her desk, and when they'd told him to mind his head getting into the Black Maria. He'd told the arresting officer, the constable on the front desk, and the custody sergeant, and so did Rory.

And he told himself it, sitting on his bunk and shaking his head over it again. It was a joke. Just a joke.

Somewhere in what they called the custody suite he heard voices and what he thought was the sound of keys, and hope fluttered irrationally to life again in him and waited briefly at his door, his eyes lifted to it.

Before he realised that it was simply someone else being detained, listening to the echo as three inches of solid reinforced cell door was banged shut, locked to the sound of keys again, and someone walked away whistling, leaving silence behind.

He wondered what Joanna and Tina were doing.

The next morning, at around eight thirty, the food flap in Phineas's cell door was unlocked and the elderly face of a custody officer peered in at him with a sort of amused curiosity, followed by a chipped white metal mug of tea and a fish paste sandwich on a paper plate.

Phineas thanked him, and then before he could close the flap again said, 'Excuse me, please, would you mind awfully telling me what's going on?' His tone was that of a respectable man finding himself in a police cell. A respectable man, and a reasonable one, but not one with limitless patience.

'I mean, frankly, this is ridiculous. It was—'

The custody officer held up a hand, as if stopping the traffic. 'Save it, son. Whatever it is, I've heard it before.'

'But it was just a joke! A stupid joke,' Phineas burst out, his face up close to the flap, to what he could see of the officer and freedom. 'We explained all that. And I have to be back in the Welsh Marches before midday, in time—'

'Back where?' the officer said, quizzically amused.

'Shrewsbury,' Phineas said, giving the nearest recognisable name on the English side of the border, something he'd had to do before, and when in Wales giving the town of Welshpool for the same reason.

'Shrewsbury! Blimey, you must have a top-drawer brief

if you think you'll be out that early. You and your mate are stars here, son. There's only four in residence at the moment. A drunk I'm about to let out, and an old regular, our Alfie, a shoplifter, nicked in Oxford Street busy filling a list of orders he'd taken for Christmas. Then there's you two. A serious fraudster and an Irish gangster over here to shoot somebody. You're topping the bill, lad. Makes my job a bit more interesting, I can tell you. Lends a bit of colour to it, as you might say.'

'Well, can I make a phone call then?' Phineas said desperately.

'Yes, you can. If you're charged. The same as elsewhere. And like elsewhere, if you are charged, then you can arrange for someone to bring in a change of clothes, and washing and shaving gear, and that, so you can look as respectable as anybody else on Monday, everybody being equal under the law.'

'Monday?'

'Your remand hearing at Bow Street. And if you've got no one to bring in these things they'll be provided for you. OK?'

'And when do we know if we're going to be charged or not?'

The officer looked at him. 'This is not your first nicking, lad, surely?'

'Well, yes, it is, actually. I've been locked up before but only for being drunk.'

'You have had a good run. Well, you can't be charged until you've been interviewed. And you can't be interviewed until, as I understand it, certain enquiries have been made, both here and in Ireland. And if they then think there's a reasonable chance of putting a court file together for the DPP, you'll be seen under caution and with legal representation. Either your own brief or a duty solicitor provided by us. OK?' He smiled helpfully. 'Any more questions? Only the other teas are getting cold.'

'No – yes! Yes, there is. You said there's just four of us here. Well, what happened to the big chap that was picked up with us, Phil somebody, with the matching floral shirt and tie?'

'Ah, you mean Phil the Neck, on account he's hardly got any. He's another star. But H Division in the East End have got him. His arrest was the work of their undercover man, the one that had you two lifted along with him. He was what the raid was about. Phil went on the trot to the Costa del Sol, holing up at the home of another well-known face, another East End villain. Came back to pay his old mum a visit on her birthday, and somebody picked the phone up. Well he won't need suntan oil where he's going. He's down for a murder. Went south of the river and took a rival gangster off the board with a pair of nostrils, as they call a—'

'Yes, I know,' Phineas said absently, 'a shotgun.'

'Honestly,' the officer said with a laugh. 'You people! Still, where would we be without you, that's what I say. I'd be out of a job for one. Enjoy your breakfast,' he added cheerily, and closed the flap.

Phineas sat on his bunk with his mug of pale tea and fish paste sandwich and was without hope.

The other East End villain living on the Costa del Sol was, of course, Frankie Mitcham. Of course it was. This was life, with its occasional malice, either by coincidence, or in his case, he was in a mood to believe, design, tying up the loose ends, and delivering him in one neat, tidy package to fate.

Put Frankie together with Phil the Neck, Eddie Carter and the company they were keeping in the Weighed Off, and add the undercover officer's report about Rory the Irish gunman, and Anne Hathaway's cottage, and the answer is enough for a remand on Monday, and the dock at the Old Bailey. He should have gone to live in Hackney with Les's mum.

And if they felt there may not be enough evidence, circumstantial, inferred, or otherwise, then, as Eddie Carter knew, there's always the fit-up, as advertised among the other cell graffiti.

A Notice From The Management. Don't worry if you feel that we don't have enough evidence to substantiate a charge or charges against you — we'll provide it.

That he was a crime novelist and Rory an actor and a resident of London, not Dublin, wouldn't get in their way for longer than five minutes. They weren't remotely famous, with the protection of lawyers and media spotlight. All they had to offer was the truth. But as Rory had said on another occasion, why spoil a good tale for the sake of that.

All he could do now for the Hall, for his friends, his dear old friends, who had never seemed more dear, nor more distant, was to tell them where Henrietta could be found, and ask them to look after Bill Sikes until he was a free man again. And suggest that meanwhile they rent out the *Cluny Belle*, at least salvage something from the wreckage of *The Ghost of Artemus Strange Experience.*

Chapter Twenty-Five

The next day, Sunday, they were allowed out in the corridor with the other inmates to stretch their legs, overseen by a custody officer sitting in a chair under the windows of the corridor with the *News of the World.*

Through the thick glass of the windows, like that in public lavatories, life was still going on in Mayfair, the muffled sound of the odd vehicle, and a glimpse of people walking past, their legs moving as if wading through water, the tip-tapping of high heels a frivolous dance of freedom.

There were now eight occupants of the cells, five of them arrested after the Saturday pubs had closed, and bearing the marks of battle to prove it. Rory, Phineas and the regular, Alfie White the shoplifter, were the old lags on the block. Phineas, out of cigarettes, was smoking one of Alfie's thin roll-ups.

If you go down, Alfie had advised him, put a few matches in a sock and make sure there's a Bible in your peter. If not you can demand one – the pages make good roll-up paper.

Rory was still in his cell, reclining on his bunk, a black Irish chieftain unbowed and contemptuous of his capturers. He had spoken to Phineas briefly in the corridor, telling him what he had to say to his eyes, gripping him by the upper arms and calling him acushla, apologising for involving him in what he called this piece of third-rate theatre, and had then retired to his cell as if to his dressing room.

Alfie was late middle-aged, small and dressed in a rumpled pinstripe suit, shirt and tie. His head was never entirely still, moving like a boxer who's not sure where the next blow's coming from, the flat of his hand cutting through the air now and then in a gesture Phineas was now familiar with.

Phineas to Alfie was obviously green, obviously new to the trade, but he admired the boldness of the stroke and had taken him under his wing.

'You've got more bleedin' front than Harrods, Phin,' he said admiringly, when first meeting him. 'And that, mate, tasty as it was, was where you went wrong, if you don't me saying so. Your mistake was to take too big a bite all at once, go for too big a job straight out.' Alfie's hand chopped the air, cutting the stroke down to size. 'I mean, I dunno how big this Anne Hathaway's gaff is, but—'

'Alfie,' Phineas said with weary patience, 'I did *not* do it!'

'I get ya, mate,' Alfie said quietly, glancing at the custody officer. 'But say for the sake of argument you did. Well in that case, I'd say that while I like to see that sort of ambition in the young, it's better to start small. Peter Pan's statue, say, in Ken Gardens. Nice and secluded, that is. Or the Albert Memorial, for a bolder stroke. That's always busy in the summer. Or even Eros in the Circus. Now there's a tasty one, my son. Always loads of tourists

189

standing around there, there is. Do a fair bit of biz there no problem, with a clipboard and the right accent. Got a bowler hat?'

'No, I'll have to invest in one,' Phineas said, resigned to not being believed whatever he said.

'Be worth it. Mind you, not that it helped Reggie Watts.'

'Who?'

'Reggie Watts. He's a mate of mine, now doing a couple of handfuls. He tried to flog Tower Bridge to a rich Yank.'

'Tower Bridge?'

'Yes, dear old Tower Bridge.'

'What, *all* of it?'

'Yes, all of it. Eyes bigger than his mouth. That's what I'm saying, see, Phin. Start small and work up.'

'Tower Bridge,' Phineas said wonderingly.

'Well, they've already got the old London Bridge over there, in Arizona, where it's making a tourist killing. Top attraction there, it is. So he was trying to push the investment angle, see. Charles St John Pawsey, Operations Executive of Her Majesty's Public Works, Bridge Division, his cards read. Bowler hat, black leather briefcase with lots of investment figures he'd made up himself in it, banker's pants, the lot. Oh, and an Old Etonian tie.'

'Oh, Old Etonian, is he?'

'Nah. Course he ain't. And that was the second mistake he made. He was wearing it, see, when he went up before London Recorder Sir James Fennington-Hore, the most senior permanent judge in the Bailey. Thought it would work like the dodgy handshakes the Freemasons use. Poor sod. If he could have afforded a proper brief he'd have had his card marked.'

'Yes, some Old Etonians can get frightfully worked up over that sort of thing,' Phineas said absently, distracted by hope, finding himself perhaps on the right side of things for once, wearing the right sort of tie, even if he didn't actually have one to wear. The undercover officer would surely make mention of school when he gave his evidence, quoting Rory's remarks in the Weighed Off.

Eton, he considered, had done little for him. And he had done even less for Eton. He was determined to be perfectly fair about that, in the Eton way. But perhaps now a sort of reconciliation might be made. Perhaps judge and defendant might meet in a shared memory of the old light blue. The boyish trebles in Chapel lifted in the 'Carmen Etonense', the dear old school set to music, its ancient, mellow red brick, and the mists of memory on the hallowed fields of autumn, fields on which it was said Waterloo was won. And the fourth of June, when it was always jolly boating weather, and there were strawberries and champagne when the shade was off the trees, and one wore a boater decked with flowers.

'Oh, yes,' he went on, buoyantly, 'that sort of thing can get steam coming out of the ears of some of the old boys who knew the place. And quite right, too, in my opinion!' he added, as one of the old boys.

Alfie laughed. 'Well, Reggie certainly didn't know it. He went to Perkins Street Secondary Modern, same as me. But it wasn't that. His mistake was wearing an Eton tie at all. In front of that particular judge.'

'Why?' Phineas asked, and almost at the same time suspecting why, the chill hand of unease touching his spine. 'Rugby?' he suggested hopefully. Then, 'Harrow...?

Not the other place? Not Harrow?' he said weakly.

'Yeah, you've got it, Phin. Harrow. Old Jimmy went to Harrow. Like Winston Churchill. And there's a lot of argy, lot of rivalry, between the two schools, I'm told.'

'Oh,' Phineas said, 'bitter. Bitter rivalry.'

'And the other thing about the old man is that he suffers with piles something rotten. Purgatory, they are some days. I was on the public pews with Reggie's sister when Reggie came up the steps, a lamb to the bleedin' slaughter, wearing his Old Etonian tie. Grinning away and winking when he spotted us, as if he was gonna see us in the Magpie afterwards. Then he saw the expression on his lordship's boat and the holiday was over. He's caught him on one of his air-cushion days, hasn't he.'

'For his lordship's – er…?' Phineas suggested delicately.

'Yeah, that's right. The coals of 'ell, they are then. And did poor old Reggie ever cop an earful after the guilty came in. Old Jimmy shifting about on the bench, glaring and snarling at him as if his rear was Reggie's fault, laying into him about him trying to sell off the nation's heritage and all that sort of thing, you know?'

Phineas nodded gloomily. 'Yes, I do know, Alfie,' he said, bowing to the inevitable, to what fate had lined up for him. 'Historical association and cultural worth, that sort of thing.'

'Yeah, stuff like that. He'd have hung him if he could. Sent him to the topping shed in Wandsworth. Used to make his day, that did, when he had a black cap job. He used to arrange it just so on his wig, taking his time over it, while peering down at the poor geezer in the dock, spinning out the agony, see. I remember when—'

'Yes – but what happened to poor old *Reggie,* Alfie?' Phineas said, desperate for some idea of what he himself might expect.

'Well, after old Jimmy's rant about the historical heritage stuff, and all that, he then took a pop at this Eton school he thought Reggie had gone to. Said something about not being entirely surprised, coming from that place. But that it gave him no pleasure seeing him bringing the school into such dire disrepute.' Alfie chuckled. 'I remember that. Dire disrepute. I liked that, dire—'

'So what did—?'

'Well, then he gets into a confab with his chief clerk, like they do, asking him how much he can give him, like. Then looking disappointed at the answer, weighs poor Reggie off with a cock and hen.'

'A cock and hen?' Phineas got out, knowing that whatever it meant he was not going to like it.

'A ten, a ten stretch. He's in the Scrubs as we speak, putting plastic animals in little bags for cereal boxes. That's where big time for Reggie, with his bowler and briefcase, ended up. But the thing is, Phin – the thing is, if he listens for once in his life, he'll come out a wiser man.'

'Ready to put the past behind him,' Phineas said, immediately seeing the wisdom in that, after even his short time behind a door, and with the prospect of a much longer stretch of it waiting for him.

'Yeah. Yeah, that's right. Ready to get on with it, to move forward. No excuse not to, see, inside. There's a wealth of knowledge on the landings, anything from the wrinkles in my game to the dos and don'ts of con tricks and armed blags. If he uses his nut and pays attention he'll come out with an education on the taxpayer. And that's what I suggest you do, Phin. Make your bird work for you, mate, know what I mean? And if you do go up in front of old Jimmy, and the chances are of course you will, as he's a permanent judge, stand on me, my son, and don't try and come any of that "not guilty" nonsense. He likes to get off early.'

Detective Inspector Eric Rawlings had been a member of the CID for over twenty years. And in those years he had been involved in several fit-ups of suspects. But always as far as he was concerned in a fair manner, always fitting-up some villain with the sort of crime he was known for, and one he'd been getting away with for far too long. And one who, as the saying went, was 'due'. Someone had to pay, the figures had to be tidied up, and it was their turn.

It was a time when the criminal and the police met in a sort of mutual understanding, if a grudging one on the criminal's part. But at least he knew that he wasn't being overcharged, that it was the sort of price in terms of a sentence he'd have to pay if he had actually done the crime.

And for a short while, the inspector, skilled at the game, had pondered ways in which Phineas and Rory might be fitted-up, if only to teach them a lesson.

It hadn't taken him long to realise that they weren't villains as he knew villains. They were the sort of public who were neither one thing nor the other, neither respectable nor criminal, and in their case the sort who were more careless than most of the line between the two. Their fingerprints had come back negative, but his hope had been that for whatever reason they had strayed over that line, maybe even for the first time, but in a rather serious way. That they had actually committed the crimes boasted of in the Weighed Off club.

But after a day's solid enquiries that had bounced from London to Dublin, from Stratford-upon-Avon to Batch Magna, that had visited Eddie Carter and, using their real names and the names used in the club, had consulted the files of the Old Bailey and Her Majesty's Diplomatic Service, and even, in a last frustrated attempt to find a bit of thread to start pulling at, the Policia Municipal on the Costa del Sol, he'd let them go. He'd had to let them go.

But he gave them more of his time before they went, that time that could have been used in the pursuit of crime that had actually happened.

He wanted to make sure that they knew something before they left. He wanted them to understand that if at *any* time in the future they got up to their jokey ways again on his manor, he would consider them 'due'.

And as they obviously didn't know what that meant, he told them in a parting shot not to worry. They'll know it when it happened to them.

They couldn't make Eddie Carter's yard before he locked the gates on Monday, and so stayed the night in Rory's one-bedroom flat off the Fulham Palace Road, retiring after a drink locally and a fish and chip supper, eaten on the way back out of sheets of yesterday's *Sunday Express*.

Phineas slept on the sofa, willingly, happily, even if he didn't have a blonde called Tina on it with him, and even though his feet were cold, stuck out over the end of it, seeing that it wasn't a cell bunk.

He had phoned the Hall when they arrived at the flat, and spoke to Clem when she answered, explaining the phone call they'd received from West End Centre police station, managing to suggest that the real reason for their detainment there was that the Metropolitan police, in the person of a certain detective inspector, had absolutely no sense of humour.

Rory then took the phone to take the blame, and to apologise for the shooting brake not turning up on Saturday. As the trip had been undertaken on the Hall's behalf, Clem said that she could hardly complain about the inconvenience it had caused, while at the same time managing to sound as if she were doing just that.

Rory swore to her there and then that they would make it up to them, that by the time they had finished the punters would be queuing up the drive of the Hall, clutching the entrance fee for *The Ghost of Artemus Strange Experience*.

Rory apologised again the next morning, when they arrived at Eddie Carter's yard, for involving him in it, and Eddie told him to forget it.

'Like old times,' he'd said, 'finding a couple of Bill on the doorstep. I think Rita felt a bit like that, as well. She offered to make them a cuppa. Never done that before.'

Rory would have bought a bottle of Bell's for the old Eddie by way of thanks for his help. But as the new Eddie no longer drank, and had never smoked, it was a box of chocolates for Rita.

'Ah, she will be pleased. She sends her love. And says when you get back you're to come and eat with us.'

'Every man should have a Rita in their lives,' Rory told Phineas. 'It was Eddie's great good fortune that she walked into his, and not somebody else's.'

'You can say that again, son,' Eddie said, beaming her worth at him.

Walking them to the shooting brake to see them off, Eddie said, 'I was gonna visit the club, after the Bill had left. You know, drop in, see if I could find anything out, like, as of course they didn't tell us much. But Rita said best leave it.' He looked at Rory as if waiting to be told otherwise.

'Well, she's right, Eddie, isn't she,' Rory said, opening the passenger door.

'Yeah,' Eddie said. 'Yeah, I know she is.'

He stood watching the brake pull away, stood watching them leave, as he had watched them leave on Friday afternoon, standing there still in his yard after they had disappeared.

Chapter Twenty-Six

Miss Wyndham, after deciding, finally, that she was going to do it, stood in front of the dressing table in her bedroom, fingering the rings on her left hand in anguished indecision.

And then, in sudden defiance of herself, of guilt and a feeling that she was being foolish, old and foolish, deluded even, her face warmed with what she was doing, she removed the rings.

She put them with the care given to ceremony in the rosewood box on her dressing table, put them away with the other memories from that past, his letters from France, from a war, and the medals, bright with polish. The Mons Star, telling of the battle in which he had fallen, and the Military Cross, awarded for gallantry, the story of how he had died.

His signet ring had been given to her by his parents. She'd had the band adjusted and had worn it on the little finger of her left hand, as he had, next to her engagement ring, all the years since.

She put on other rings to cover the bareness of those fingers, and then her cape, and green felt hat with a jay's bright feather in the band, and when the doorbell went opened the door to Rupert.

They were going to dinner in Phan-glas, a small market town a twenty-minute drive into Wales. They were sharing a first experience, the first time either of them had eaten an Indian meal. The restaurant had been suggested to Rupert by Phineas, who was a regular there, and Rupert had booked a taxi from Mr Morris, who ran a one-man service from Little Batch, a sister village three miles downriver.

Mr Morris carried no sign on his highly polished car that it served as a taxi. The only indication that he was other than a private driver when working was the black peaked hat, the company's badge removed from it, that he'd worn with the rest of the uniform before retiring from a career as a bus driver. His bus had usually been the 49, a single-decker Miss Wyndham used regularly in and out of Kingham.

It was the first time she'd been in his taxi, and when greeting him Miss Wyndham would not normally have failed to notice the hat. Notice it and wonder if larceny had been involved. If Mr Morris, a respected figure in the area, a parish councillor, whose daughter was headmistress of Batch Magna primary school, and wife a fellow member of the WI, hadn't taken it away with him when he left, along with, perhaps, a clock, and a little joke about timetable schedules, and the managing director's good wishes for a happy retirement.

Miss Wyndham would have noticed, and would have had something to say about it, if only to herself, and then her cats, until a wider audience was available. A piece of gossip, a small note from somebody else's life, to give her own a brief, second-hand meaning.

But this was a different Miss Wyndham, sitting in the back of the taxi with Rupert. She was no longer old Miss Wyndham, gossip and spinster of this village, but simply Harriet Wyndham, a woman.

The maître d' was also the son of the house, the restaurant a family affair, waiters and kitchen staff, his mother and father the chefs.

When he took their topcoats Rupert mentioned that Phineas Cook had recommended them. The maître d' laughed and shook his head, as if just told a joke, and led them, chuckling, to their table.

'Harriet, you look, if I may say so, charming,' Rupert said, taking his tone from the occasion, from a table for two laid with starched linen and polished plate.

'Thank you, Rupert,' Miss Wyndham said, her cheeks warming again for the second time that day.

She had on her Lovat Harris tweed suit with a pine green velvet collar, over a white frilly blouse, and a jade necklace that had belonged to her mother.

After being guided through the large menu by the maître d', the table was busy with servings of lamb korma and chicken tikka, Bombay potatoes, saffron rice, spring rolls and papadums, chapattis, samosas and onion bhajis, and glasses of white wine for Miss Wyndham and chilled lager for Rupert.

Both of them sampling each other's orders, and commenting on new discoveries in the side dishes. And sharing a discreet giggle at an overweight man in a party at a table opposite, napkin tucked businesslike into his shirt collar, his face, plump as a pudding, steaming gently over the fire of whatever he had on his plate.

'A Turkish bath while you eat,' Rupert whispered to Miss Wyndham, who had to hide a fresh outbreak of giggling in her napkin.

She felt as if she were on holiday, in some place far away from that past she had lived with all these years. He was reminding her of someone she had only a vague memory of, set in time, and it was as if that someone had both returned and had never been away.

When the bill was presented by the maître d', smiling as if apologising for having to introduce a note of commerce into the evening, Miss Wyndham reached down for her handbag at the foot of her chair.

Rupert shook his head and said gently, 'Please don't.'

When they left, the maître d' saw them off as if their patronage had saved the restaurant and family from bankruptcy.

Rupert said that the deliciousness of the food aside, it was easy to see why almost every table was taken.

They decided on a drink first before ringing Mr Morris, at a pub on a corner down from the restaurant called The Y Ddraig Arms, its sign, with a red dragon on it ready for flight, moving in winds that had picked up, carrying rain on them.

They sat with their drinks by a log fire gathering ash, while the gusts of wind and rain beat at a casement window behind the drawn curtains.

Miss Wyndham had white wine again, Rupert a pint of Black Boy bitter.

The Black Boy, she was able to tell him, was the original name of Batch Magna's Steamer Inn.

'It was built,' she said, regarding him across the table, the evening adding a brightness like mischief to her eyes, 'after the head of the joyless Oliver Cromwell had been spiked on Westminster Bridge, to deter other would-be revolutionaries. And called The Black Boy, and the bitter of that name brewed there, in honour of a monarch, their young monarch, Charles the Second, who had come home. And then Humph's great uncle, Sir Cosmo Strange, brought the paddle steamers to Batch Magna all the way from the waters of the River Thames. And the name was changed in celebration of that. But its bitter is still called Black Boy. D'you see?' she added, lesson over.

'I see,' Rupert said with a laugh.

He lifted his glass and drank to the Black Boy and Sir Cosmo. 'And,' he added, 'to us.'

She waited for a moment, a moment that seemed to have gathered in her chest, that did something to her breathing.

And then, when he said no more, merely smiled at her, she said, 'To us,' and laughed suddenly and briefly at nothing, and having never been drunk before wondered if she was.

She lifted her glass to drink, and then said, 'I was engaged once. Have I told you that?'

He nodded gravely. 'Yes, Hattie, you did.'

'His name was Arthur,' she said, as if he hadn't spoken. 'He died in France, in 1914. Almost as soon as the war started. But of course I've told you that. How stupid of me.'

Rupert, breaking a silence between them, said, as if answering a question she'd asked, 'I was born on a farm. My parents had a farm, a mixed farm, near the village of Hamley in Warwickshire. That's where I was taught to lay a Midland bullock hedge.'

He paused. Miss Wyndham waited, all ears.

'I was one of six children. I left the village school at fourteen to work for Dad. I remember having to leave a nest-warm bed on winter mornings when it was still dark and there was ice on the water troughs, and the heat and dust of summer in the hay fields. We had a team of five Shires, sweet, big old boys. They could pull anything, and mow ten acres of grass in a day. I can still smell their stables, hear them blowing, and stamping their feet against the feather mites they got sometimes. Still feel their warmth and the smell of the harness...'

Rupert seemed to have wandered off, and Miss Wyndham prompted him. 'Are any of your family still alive? Your siblings, I mean?'

'I don't know,' he said simply. 'I left home at sixteen and never went back. I wrote Mum and Dad a letter and just walked away one morning. I went to Kenilworth looking for work, and saw an army recruiting office. I thought, that will do. When I told the recruiting sergeant my age, he said, 'Go outside, have a couple of quick birthdays, then come back in.' They got two and six for each new recruit. And so there I was, Private Ainsworth of the Ninth Battalion, the Royal Warwickshire Regiment. And a year later we left to fight the Turks in Gallipoli.'

He paused, the name of the place like a full stop in his eyes. And then went on, quietly, 'Gallipoli went badly for us. We lost an entire company there in one battle, along with other losses.'

He left out the rest of it. He left out seeing death for the first time in the eyes of the life he took with a bayonet, a lad of around his own age. He left out the furnace heat, the lack of fresh water, the body lice, the stench, and the corpse flies swarming on what little food they had before it reached their mouths, and the spread of disease from death rotting out in no-man's land.

And he left out a memory that had followed him for years. The cries of those left to die out in no-man's land, that had to be left to die, because of the efficiency of the Turkish snipers. Youths stripped of everything but their true age, hearing that in their screams of pain, and their calling, over and over, for their mothers.

'How dreadful,' Miss Wyndham said. 'How dreadful war is. Will we, I wonder, ever learn?'

Rupert appeared to consider it, then shook his head. 'No. No, Hattie, I have to say that I don't think we will. Only get better at it. And perhaps, with the growing use of technology, learn to distance ourselves from it. Until we forget what it looks like close up.'

'It makes one sometimes, I confess, almost question one's faith.'

'I don't believe we can blame God. He gave us free will. I see Him returning His attention to us one day, a parent coming home to the mess we've made and asking, "What have you done?"'

There was a small silence, into which Miss Wyndham softly inserted a question she'd been dying to ask for some time.

'Did you ever marry, Rupert?'

'No. No, but I – look, let's have another drink. We've time. Then I'll ring Mr Morris from here.'

Miss Wyndham reached for her handbag again. 'Only if—'

'No. No, Hattie. Tonight's my treat. Please.'

When he was up at the bar, Miss Wyndham watched a young couple sitting on their own at a nearby table with eyes only for each other, and smiled, unseen, at them. Not from memories from her past, from a time when someone had looked at her like that, but from the here and now. Sharing across the difference of the years between them the same sort of smile while waiting for Rupert.

When he returned with the drinks, he went on, 'I was never married, but I was engaged once. To a woman I met while working in London, as a porter in a department store in Knightsbridge. I moved round a lot after the war. Not tramping. Just moving from job to job and living in digs. The engagement didn't work out.'

'A pity, but best surely done then,' Miss Wyndham said. 'Than when married, with perhaps children.'

'Yes,' he said, and then, as if it had something to do with a broken engagement, added, 'We were evacuated from Gallipoli the following January. Were lucky to be evacuated. We left so many behind. So many. The Battalion then saw action in Mesopotamia, Baghdad, Iraq. I was invalided out from there, from Iraq, with a head wound.'

'Oh, Rupert!' Miss Wyndham cried.

'Oh, nothing serious. Caught a bit of shrapnel. A shell splinter. But it stopped me enlisting in London when we had another war, after, that is, the war to end all wars.

Because I had blackouts of a sort, as a result of it. Not falling down or anything, just becoming sort of elsewhere for a short while. But it was on my medical notes, so that was that. I pointed out to them that I was otherwise perfectly fit. It's just that if I did wander off up there,' he said, tapping his head, 'they'd have to get on with the war without me until I got back. But it was no good. I ended up as an air raid warden for the duration.'

'Well – you had done your bit in the first lot.'

'Maybe, but I was not comfortable with other people doing my fighting for me. Anyway, after that war, I had quite a good job in Birmingham, where I'd then ended up. A supervisor in a bedding warehouse, one of a chain, with the next step up, they said, management. And then one day I decided that I simply couldn't do it any more – while not being altogether sure, as I'm still not today, what "it" was, or is. All I knew was that I had to go, had to move, and keep moving.'

Followed still for a while by memories of war, of Gallipoli, living again for him in the flames of the London Blitz, the things he had seen and heard. Followed for a while by the voices of those he had known, close pals some of them, calling from no-man's land.

He had walked through the night sometimes, trying to leave them behind. And when the time came when he was finally free of them, when he could hear them no more, their silence carried for him still guilt and recrimination, as if left behind on the wind, on all that remained of them.

Chapter Twenty-Seven

Sitting in the kitchen of Batch Hall, Phineas was talking about how pleased he'd been to get a Christmas card from Alfie White, his fellow inmate in the custody suite of West End Central.

'He simply sent it to Phin – with a F – Cook, Batch Magna, and Mrs Pugh in the post office gave it to me when I went in yesterday. Got a little robin on the front, and after wishing me happy Christmas inside it said, "One step at a time", with three exclamation marks.' He smiled fondly at the thought of it, and then said to Rory, 'Sends his best to you, by the way. He's out on bail, but expects to be inside for Christmas, doing six months. So he's sending his Christmas cards out early.'

'A good man, Alfie,' Rory said. 'Generous with his roll-ups. But he needs to try another branch of delinquency. He seems to spend more time in than out.'

'He's aware of his faults,' Phineas said defensively, 'he said he intends working on them. Alfie's a shoplifter,' he explained to the rest of the company. And when Phineas then went on to say that Alfie had been caught in Oxford Street ticking off a list of orders he'd taken for Christmas,

Humphrey wondered wildly for a moment if he did credit.

'Alfie's problem is not technique,' Rory said, 'but his looks. He's ideal casting for that sort of crime. The store detectives probably just take it in turns bagging him.'

'Well, if he does go down again this time,' Phineas said, 'I'll invite him to spend a weekend on the *Belle* when he comes out. A spot of river air, after being banged up for six months with a chamber pot.'

'Just keep him away from the shops,' Rory said.

They were taking a break from rehearsing *The Ghost of Artemus Strange Experience*, the clash of steel ringing out on the stairs and landing of that house as it had done when Artemus stood alone between the Roundhead soldiers and the women in the schoolroom, now for the purposes of the show one of the empty bedrooms on the landing where the action was to take place – for, it was hoped, an audience of twenty at three pounds a head.

Sitting with the others in the kitchen were seven re-enactors, members of the English Revolution Society, canvassed by Cuthbert Stanley, including the Captain of Horse, Kevin Thompson-Miller, an insurance loss adjuster, whose other life was a wife and two children in a suburban semi-detached in Birmingham. One of the Roundhead members, who'd broken a toe at work yesterday, had yet to be replaced. And the pregnant wife of a Cavalier had given birth, but he would, they were assured, be there next weekend.

The seven had rehearsed yesterday as well, on Saturday afternoon. Kevin, an actual Captain of Horse in the Society, had made Rory work at it when it came to the duel between the two.

Rory had found immediate disfavour in his eyes for the length of his hair and because he was an actor. Kevin had first cropped his hair in protest at the long-haired Swinging Sixties, simmering with moral outrage throughout at its hippies and free love. It was an outrage that had found release in fencing, and that zeal had taken him to county level in the sport, had won him cups and seen the authorship of a small book on Renaissance swordsmanship. His life outside work and family was now fencing, and he had dedicated that part of it to the English Revolution Society, rather than any other re-enactment group, because it was called just that.

In Kevin's opinion, another revolution of the same sort was overdue. When he put on the plain cloth and lobster-pot helmet of a Puritan soldier, he was donning more than a recreational re-enactor's uniform: he was making a statement.

Cuthbert Stanley had also found a member to play Artemus. He couldn't be there that weekend because of family reasons, but was keen to do it, and would be turning up for a first practice on the coming Saturday morning

The re-enactors had jobs to go to in the week, but the coming weekend, both Saturday and Sunday evenings, would see the first outing of *The Ghost of Artemus Strange Experience*, after a run-through on Saturday and a dress rehearsal.

They had just finished a full rehearsal and were eating a late Sunday lunch before returning to Birmingham.

After hours of athletic swordplay and heroic death, they were tucking into a casserole of venison flank with dumplings. The meat was a present from Owain Owen, who could get within ten feet of a herd of deer without spooking them, and who had been on another cull on an estate across the border.

Rupert had left earlier to put his feet under Miss Wyndham's Sunday table, roast beef on this occasion, accompanied by the delicious result of her recipe for Yorkshire pudding, and the two bottles of Black Boy bitter she had waiting for him.

They were in the sitting room now, watching the afternoon film, chuckling over *The Pink Panther* together on the sofa, the smell of Rupert's pipe in the air, and a log fire burning in the fireplace, with winter outside the windows.

For him Gallipoli was now where it belonged, honoured in memory, but in the past. And for Miss Wyndham, sitting in the house in which she had been born, that had known Arthur's voice for the last time, that had seen him smoking a rather self-conscious pipe with her father, and watched with amusement his dutiful touring of the flowerbeds with her mother, the past, that past, for her, was now also just that.

'I'll make tea when the advertisements come on,' she said.

Chapter Twenty-Eight

Rory was in the wardrobe department of the Kingham Repertory Theatre, being fitted for his costume as Captain of Cavaliers, while exchanging theatre gossip with Maggie the wardrobe mistress.

The room was busy with what it did, crowded with the things needed to do it. A large worktable strewn with pincushions, tape measures, dressmaker's shears, tailor's chalk, scissors, a sewing machine, strips of fabric, and a cheese grater and sheets of sandpaper to jump the years and put age into period costumes.

There were dressmaker's mannequins standing limbless about the room, clothing rails of costumes, signed black and white photographs on a wall of past actors with hopeful smiles. Shelves of haberdashery, shoes, underwear, hats and wigs, actors' measurement files, pots of fabric paint and paint out of which, when mixed with a delicate and skilful hand, came make-believe, came a stage world of mud, vomit, sweat and several types of blood.

Rory stood regarding himself in a tall mirror that had found a space on a wall, brushing with sweep of a Cavalier's hand at the feather in his hat. At his waist was slung a replica Cavalier's duelling rapier from the armoury, a walk-in cupboard at one end of the room.

He removed the sword from its leather scabbard and hefted it in a hand. 'Good balance. And grip. And a good true blade,' he said, looking down its length, the steel bright with reflected light.

'You've gone too far this time, Sir Percy!' he snarled then, and attacked the air with it, cutting and thrusting, and then, leg extended for a lunge to the heart, drove it home. He pulled the blade out and coolly watched his opponent slump lifeless to the ground.

He cleaned imaginary blood off it, wiping it casually on the clothing of an imaginary Sir Percy, and after returning the sword to its scabbard adjusted his hat in the mirror.

'Damn me, if the fella didn't have me in disarray.'

Maggie laughed. 'How about the boots? Is the fit all right?' she said, in a soft border accent.

Rory walked a few paces up and down. 'Yeah, fine. Maggie, look, I hope this isn't going to get you into any trouble.'

'I've told you. No problem. I'm in charge here. Besides, Phineas has given us a credit on the advertising fliers.'

Phineas had arrived at the theatre with Rory, looking for advice from the stage manager. He had found Neil, a towering Highland Scot with a shining ginger beard, in the wings, doing a crossword at the prompt desk. He wanted Neil's advice on the dry-ice machine. There were no instructions with it, so he had no idea about its working, or even where to buy dry ice.

'You can get it from the people we get ours from, Norton's Food, in Drayford,' Neil said, naming a market town a few miles away.

'Ah, yes, I've seen their vans about, with that thing on the roof,' Phineas said, his finger describing a propeller going round.

'Evaporator fan. Aye, that's them. They supply the stuff to food producers and meat processors, that kind of thing. I'll give you their details in a bit. Do you have proper containers?'

When Phineas said they had, he said, 'Pack them with newspaper or towels when you pick the ice up. It'll make it last longer. And buy blocks of ice, not pellets. That will also help it last longer, and it's cheaper. Then when you need it break it up with a hammer. And wear gloves when handling it – but not woollen ones – or use a towel or oven mitts. Or you risk frostbite. And whatever you do don't put the lid on too tight – don't seal the stuff in. It will sublimate—'

'It will what?'

'Turn into gas, laddie – carbon dioxide. Dry ice is its solid form. And if that happens, you'll get a different theatrical effect from the one you're after. *Bang.*'

'I see,' Phineas said doubtfully. 'Anything else we need to watch out for?'

Neil laughed. 'It's not nitroglycerin. It's not inflammable, and it's not normally given to exploding. Unless sealed in, and left nowhere to go. When do you open? When's your first night?'

'Saturday. This Saturday.'

'Och, man, you've days yet. Look, I have an instruction manual in the office somewhere. Why don't I dig it out, add my wee contribution to it in writing, and post it to you.'

'I can't put you to all that—'

'Och, it's nay a problem. I'll stick it in with the outgoing office post. Be with you in no time.'

'Well, in that case, allow me to whisk you away up the road. If, that is, you have time.'

'Aye, I do,' Neil said, closing the newspaper with the crossword in it. 'Let me get ma coat.'

By 'up the road' Phineas had meant the Sun pub, on the same side as the theatre, a wall in its back bar plastered with playbills and black and white photographs, including a glossy of one of Phineas's favourite actresses, Margaret Rutherford.

'Old England on a bike,' he said. 'When was she here? At the theatre?'

'Some time back now. She did a charity show for the General Hospital,' Maggie said. 'She's an absolute darling. Heart open to the world. Both she and her husband, Stringer. Smashing people. The sort we could do with more of. Cheers,' she added, lifting her pint of Guinness. A thirty-something brunette, her dark eyes seeming to simmer with secrets that kept her gently amused. Both she and Neil knew how *The Ghost of Artemus Strange Experience* had come about, the deed disinterred by Phineas from the pages of an ancient tome in Kingham reference library, and he now told them how it would be staged at the Hall.

'Four Roundheads and their captain trying to get at the women behind the door of a bedroom on the landing. The eighteen-year-old Artemus rushes to their defence. He falls to their swords. Four Royalist troopers and his father then enter the Hall, and they fight it out on the stairs and on the landing. The Roundhead troopers are dispatched. And there's a finale of a duel between the Roundhead Captain of Horse and Artemus's father, Rory here.'

'Avenging my son's death once nightly on Saturday and Sunday. I give you his bravery,' Rory added, lifting his pint in salute.

'And where does the smoke come in, the dry ice?' Neil asked.

'The women,' Phineas said, 'who have been shouting and yelling behind the door, fall silent, the landing light is switched off, and out of sight in the bathroom off the landing I start pumping in the smoke from the machine. Artemus rises first, taking up his sword again, followed by the rest. A ghostly, soundless fight, their swords touching only the air.'

'Och, that sounds fine. 'Tis a pity I'm working on Saturday. And Sunday's ma darts night. I'm in a local team.'

'I'm going. Phineas is picking me up, aren't you, chuck,' Maggie said, tweaking his cheek. 'And I've warned him not to stand me up this time for a police cell. Even if it is in the West End.'

'Men!' Neil said.

Maggie talked then about another actor whose photograph was on the pub wall. A former star of a TV soap who had appeared at the rep in a touring play. A man of small height and immense ego.

'A diva in trousers,' she said, and shrugged. 'But his name brought the soap fans in. They were queuing at the stage door nightly afterwards.'

'An insufferably rude, arrogant man,' Neil said. 'His conceit an elephant that brought forth onstage the presence and talent the size of a mouse.'

Maggie laughed at a memory. 'Neil threatened to pee on his head, when he kept pestering him during a tech.'

'A technical rehearsal,' Rory translated for Phineas.

'Well, he's got the height for it,' Phineas said. 'Have you actually peed on anyone's head before, Neil?'

'No, but I was willing to give it a go with that man. One of the monsters of ego we have in our trade. They spend years feeling inadequate, for good reason. Then they're made to feel special. It goes to their tiny heads.'

'Talking about big egos and small talent,' Rory said, and shared a memory of watching a film about Anne Frank in a Dublin cinema, the part played by a film star known more for her demands off set than her talent on.

'Something of course that the Dublin audience picked up almost as soon as she opened her mouth. All Dubliners are critics of acting – Dublin's a stage, and they're on every day. And she was so bad that when the Germans broke in looking for her, a shout went up telling them she was in the attic.'

Neil, addressing himself to Phineas and Rory, then said, 'It's just struck me, lads. Not, I hope, being alarmist, but I think it's better perhaps you should know about Councillor Simpkins.'

'Ah, yes,' Maggie said. 'The unlovely Mr Simpkins.'

'Obersturmführer Simpkins is a strutting, pettifogging jack-in-office with a clipboard and the authority of the county council behind him. He is the recently elected councillor for sports, recreation and entertainment, with special responsibility, when it comes to the last, for health and safety. Six months back, he cost the theatre the price of a new iron, a new fire curtain, with of course new operating gear. Not cheap. He's already closed down a disco club on safety grounds, and made a wine bar put in an emergency exit, even though all the customers and staff had to do was to walk out of the door onto the street.'

'And he has accidentally-on-purpose roving hands, and a bad wig,' Maggie added. 'Looks like roadkill without the gore.'

'And you think what, Neil?' Phineas said.

'Well, I'm not sure what I think. I mean, it may not apply to you at all. I just thought—'

'Surely it doesn't,' Rory said. 'Batch Hall's a private house.'

'I'm not too sure about that,' Phineas said. 'They run it as a guest house. And it has drinks and gaming licences, both issued by the county council.'

'A gaming licence?' Neil said. 'What, dinner jackets and a roulette wheel in a back room? When it comes to making money out of their bricks and mortar the English aristocracy simply cannot be beaten.'

'Fruit machines, Neil,' Phineas told him. 'Bought second-hand from an amusement arcade in Rhyll.'

'You disappoint me, Phineas. But dinna fash yersels. There's a big difference between our venue and what you're doing. How many are you catering for?'

'Twenty. We worked it out that that is the most we can get away with, in terms of people being able to see what's going on. Because the staircase, though wide, has a curve in it. We had to take a grandfather clock off the half-landing, because they'll sort of have to follow the action up the stairs when the Royalists storm in to the rescue, and watch the rest from there.' He looked at Neil with a slightly anxious air.

'They canna expect the stalls or dress circle for three quid,' Neil briskly reassured him. 'And the play's the thing, you know.'

'That's what Rory said.'

'And yon Rory is right.'

'We'll give them the heat and clash of battle to keep their minds off things,' Rory said.

'And a free coffee and hotdog,' Phineas added.

'Och, well, there you are then,' Neil said, as if that settled it. 'And as regards Adolf Simpkins, as I said – there's a big difference in an audience of twenty and our two hundred and fifty, which is what the wee man based his findings on, a full house.'

'A full house. I've heard about those,' Maggie said.

'Aye, well, lassie, the numbers are looking good for the panto, Jill tells me.'

'What are you doing?' Rory asked.

'*Cinderella* again,' Maggie said.

'It puts bums on seats, Maggie. The management line,' Neil said.

'You shall go to the ball,' Phineas said. 'We all want a bit of that in our lives.'

Chapter Twenty-Nine

Artemus Strange, as embodied by Nigel Driver, was a young trainee solicitor in a law practice in the city of Birmingham, of average height, willowy build, and fair haired and blue eyed in the English way. He was also a competitive club fencer with rapier and sabre.

For Phineas, he belonged, or would one day, with those who made the rules, which included not only solicitors, particularly those specialising in divorce, but school masters, bank managers, public officials of all sorts, and now police inspectors.

He knew that what they did had to be done because that is how society worked. He knew that, and he knew that it wouldn't do for everyone to be like him, he knew that as well. He'd been told both things enough times, by different people, over the years. And he was grateful, in a vague sort of way, that those things were being done. That there were people perfectly happy to do them, perfectly happily building lives doing them. Working away at whatever it was while he, as it were, gazed on at nothing very much in particular out of a window.

And on Friday, as it wasn't for one reason or another

convenient for anyone else at the Hall to do so, he had volunteered to drive to Shrewsbury to pick Nigel up.

Nigel had phoned earlier in the day to ask if he could come that evening, instead of Saturday morning. His car was currently in a local garage with a wiring problem, and a work colleague, he'd explained, was driving to Shrewsbury for the weekend to meet his girlfriend's parents, and had offered him a lift. He had been told that the Hall could put him up until Sunday, when he'd arranged the same lift back after the show.

He was told to ask his colleague to drop him off at the railway station and to watch out for a yellow sports car.

And when Phineas met him there, in front of the station, there was something about the way he wore his youth that reminded him of his son, Daniel. Who, mysteriously to his father, had recently been awarded a research fellowship into something called applied mathematics.

And talking to Nigel on the drive back to Batch Magna, he found that he liked him. Liked someone who would one day be a solicitor – liked someone who *wanted* to be a solicitor.

Liked him enough to listen to him, not just pretend to, when, over a meal at the Hall, he talked about his intended speciality, corporate finance. Even encouraging him to enlarge on it in the pub afterwards by asking him questions about it, Nigel enthusiastically going into detail about company law procedures, divestitures, mergers, acquisitions and something called private equity finance. Phineas not understanding any of it, but listening with the fondness of a parent to a son who did.

He even visited, as it were, Nigel in his future life, in a

pleasant detached house in a small park of manicured lawns and matching flower beds. Saw several scrubbed children tumbling out onto the drive in school uniforms, the weekend golf clubs waiting in the hall, the black tie Rotary evenings, the quiet smiles he exchanged with his pretty young wife at one of their dinner parties, a language of their own speaking of the successful life they had made together.

The next morning Phineas was directing a run-through for the first full showing of *The Ghost of Artemus Strange Experience.* He would be acting as narrator, explaining the background to the attack and the following action to the audience – which so far amounted to ten. It was hoped more would book by phone, or turn up and pay at the door.

'Nigel,' Phineas said, standing with him on the upper landing and wagging a finger at a bedroom door directly opposite the staircase. 'This evening, Clem, with Annie and Shelly, will be behind that door kicking up a racket. They would have heard the banging on the front doors down there, heard the enemy trying to get in – though actually it will be Humph. Who, when it comes to hitting things, is easily a match for five Ironheads – and have barricaded themselves in the schoolroom, served for our purposes by this bedroom. That is your cue to come to the rescue, OK?'

'OK, Phin,' Nigel said, dressed like the other actors in his street clothes, but holding the rapier that last night had arrived strapped to his suitcase. 'What happens, incidentally,' he wanted to know, 'if it's raining, pouring with rain?'

'Then we lose a nice dramatic start, because both Roundheads and Cavaliers would then have to lurk in the kitchen. And let's hope it doesn't rain, because it might put people off.'

'And the spectators will stand down there, will they, Phin, on the stairs and half landing?' Nigel said, sounding doubtful.

'The audience, Nigel. Call them the audience. It will help get you into play mode. Yes, that's where they'll stand. And yes, I know it will be a bit awkward, a bit cramped. But it gives the feel of the drama actually happening, of being part of it, rather than watching when sitting down.'

'Well, yes, I suppose so. It's just that it all looks a bit...'

'And they're getting a free coffee and hotdog, you know.'

'Oh, well,' Nigel said vaguely.

'Now,' Phineas went on, 'when you respond to the distress of the women you do not hesitate. You could be forgiven for doing so, at aged eighteen and with five hairy, battle-hardened soldiers intent on spoils to confront. But you do not hesitate. You rush, sword in hand, to the rescue, brave lad that you are.'

He leaned over the landing banister and called down then to the Roundhead re-enactors waiting in the hall.

'Kevin, you and your Roundhead troopers have just broken in through the doors. You hear female voices and charge up the stairs. Right, off you go. Well, come on, Kevin – *charge*. You're on your way to rape and pillage, not going to bed!'

That evening, Phineas would tell those gathered for the entertainment, and their free hotdog and coffee, that the Roundheads charging up the stairs are met by the scion of the house, eighteen-year-old Artemus Strange. Who, in defence of the womenfolk in the barricaded schoolroom, puts up an heroic fight, before falling, wounded, but not fatally, to their swords. The Cromwellian Captain of Horse, wearing the red sash of an officer, delivers the coup de grâce, as befits Artemus's rank of gentleman. And then, through the same front doors that have yielded to the enemy, bursts Sir Richard Strange with some of his king's men, the main body of Royalists having put the Roundheads to rout at Batch Castle. They charge up the stairs and there, on the landing, Sir Richard learns the price his young son has paid for his bravery.

'Right – Rory, now your turn,' Phineas called, giving him and his Cavaliers their cue, and then, peering down at the hall, found it empty.

'Rory! where the hell are you!' he yelled.

'Wait there, please,' he said to Kevin and his Roundheads.

'Perhaps our film star's still in his dressing room, drinking champagne,' Kevin said.

'That sort of remark, Kevin,' Phineas said, 'does not help matters.'

'Yes, well,' Kevin muttered.

'Can I get up, Phin?' Nigel asked politely.

'What? Well, yes, you might as well I suppose, Nigel. I'll go and see where they've got to.'

Rory was in the kitchen, sitting across the long pine table from Jasmine.

Humphrey looked up from a morning newspaper. 'How's it going, Phin? Sounds swell from here.'

'Well, it's all a bit one-sided, frankly, Humph, at the moment,' he said, looking pointedly at Rory. 'All

Roundheads and no Cavaliers. May I ask what you're doing, Rory?' he enquired mildly.

'Having my tea leaves read, Phin,' Rory said, not taking his eyes off Jasmine, who was staring into a mug he'd had tea in.

'It's called tasseomancy, Phineas,' Annie said. 'Jasmine can read the leaves like a book, she can. She's told me a few things, I can tell you. Past, present and future. Told me that our Bryony was pregnant before even she knew it. And about the old floor going through in the Land Rover.'

Phineas wasn't listening. He was shaking his head at what he was looking at. Rory and two of his troopers sitting at the table with their tea, and the other two Cavaliers hopefully feeding the fruit machines.

He was about to comment, to come out with something biting, when Jasmine, her professional voice rising in a vision, declaimed, 'I see an ocean. I see a large ocean. I see you crossing it. Heading towards the horizon and a bright sun which seems to beckon.'

'What's that mean?' Rory asked, his tone suggesting that he was hoping it meant what he thought it meant.

'The leaves say that you are about to enter a more successful period of your life. But in another place, another land, across the other side of an ocean.'

Rory slapped the table. 'I knew it! Hollywood. She's talking about Hollywood,' he told Phineas. 'By ship. I dislike flying.'

'Well, bully for you,' Phineas said. 'Absolutely splendid. Couldn't happen to a nicer chap. But may I remind you, you and your merry men here, that you're supposed to be charging to Nigel's rescue? And that we're all waiting for you up there?'

'Ah, come on, Phineas,' Rory said. 'We know what to do. I mean, it's hardly five-act Shakespeare, is it.'

Shelly and Clem were making the morning sandwich run, but Humphrey was there, and Phineas indicated him as representing the family and their obligations to it, the promises they had made.

'Is that the right attitude to take, Rory?' he asked gently, a spiritual adviser inviting him to seek the answer in his own conscience. 'It isn't, as you say, Shakespeare. Nor yet the lead on a London stage. And it's a long way from the glamour and riches of Hollywood, I know, but this little—'

Rory lifted his hands in surrender. 'OK, OK! You win. And you are right, Phineas. You are right,' he said, a man rising to the occasion, and doing so upstage of Phineas. 'There are, as Stanislavski pointed out, no small parts, only small actors. And let it not be said of me that I am a small actor. Come, gentlemen of the king,' he said to his troopers. 'To war. And do I cross your palm with silver, or something, Jas?' he added.

'Not in this kitchen,' Jasmine said. 'You're a friend here in this kitchen. But don't forget us when you get to Hollywood. And snog Paul Newman for me when you do get there.'

'Done. Apart from snogging Paul Newman, that is. And while I'm waiting for the call, how about if I buy you a drink at lunchtime?'

Chapter Thirty

They had a dress rehearsal in the afternoon, and the past lived again there. Artemus Strange in doublet, lace ruffs and cuffs, stockings and bright embroidered garters, and the cries and clash of steel as Roundheads and Royalists met under its roof again in battle.

And they had their first audience for it, an invited audience of river and village people, Jasmine Roberts bringing the youngest members of her family with her, and Priny and the Commander bringing a couple of friends who were visiting. The Owens were there, Bryony Owen with her family, and her friends, and Ffion Owen and her new boyfriend, and friends of theirs, and Sion, her eldest brother, brought his friends from the rugby club, turning up with them from the pub with bottles, children and dogs running around the crowded hall and kitchen.

They cheered when Rory and his men triumphed, as if a win by their local football team. Whether they knew the history of it or not, they were all Royalists, all Cavaliers, at heart, in that daft and happy place, that land which sits between two countries and belongs wholly to neither.

But where men had taken sides in the Civil War, and fought to keep an English king on the throne, and when summer came again after Cromwell's Puritan winter, and the bells rang out in London to welcome a young monarch restored from exile, they planted oak trees and built an inn, a house of laughter and song, in his name, and called it, and the first brew made there, The Black Boy, the affectionate nickname for Charles II.

A few of the people invited for the dress rehearsal were still there that evening when the first showing of *The Ghost of Artemus Strange Experience* started at the publicised time of eight o'clock. They had had twelve bookings, three of those from the village. And there was room, just, for everyone else, because four of the nine that had booked elsewhere had simply not bothered to turn up.

Sion would have stayed on anyway, to operate the dry-ice machine to pump out the ghostly smoke for the Dance of the Fallen, as the fliers, penned by Phineas, had put it. It had been decided that he should do it, rather than Phineas, who would have to clamber over the same fallen at the end of the sword fight to reach the bathroom and the machine.

The machine was on an extension lead plugged into a socket outside the bathroom. Sion had filled it with water a quarter of an hour before the start of the show, which had been timed at around forty-five minutes. The time it took, according to the handbook Neil the stage manager had sent on, for the water to reach the right temperature for the dry ice.

As Phineas went into his narrative in the hall below, Sion

settled down on a chair in the doorway of the bathroom, as if in a box seat, to watch the show with a glass and a bottle of cider.

A show which started with the thunder of Humphrey's fists on one of the Hall's double front doors, before it crashed open, the Roundhead Captain of Horse and his men pausing in the hall at the sound of females in the house. And then charging up the stairs, the three women in the bedroom, after taking their cue from Humphrey banging on the door, starting to yell for help.

The Roundheads were met by Artemus, rushing to the rescue from another part of upstairs, heedless of his own safety. His sword a brave flight of bright steel, halting the soldiers' advance, driving them back. And then dispatching one of them with a neat thrust to the heart, before falling himself, first to the blades of the troopers, and then, fatally, to that of an officer.

The Captain then turned his attention to the prizes behind the bedroom door, ordering his men to break it down. An attempt had been made, resulting in more yelling from inside, when Richard and his king's men arrived at the Hall, and drawing their swords pounded up the stairs. There was a brief, fierce exchange of steel, which saw off the remaining three Roundhead troopers, and left a Cavalier among the dead.

It was rehearsed so that the five bodies did not litter the landing and get under the feet of the duellists at the end of the scene. All five were sprawled in positions on the top stairs, even the one felled by Artemus on the landing, who had to pretend he had arrived there in a state of wounded confusion.

The bedroom door was opened by one of the Cavaliers still standing, and the three women slipped out and joined the three of them in the corridor, out of sight of the audience below, leaving the landing to the duellists.

The fight, the war, reduced to two men, Monarchist and Parliamentarian facing each other, as if for the divided soul of England.

Facing each other in the middle of a circle of light on an empty stage, as Rory saw it, their seconds watching silently from the stone shadows of a castle wall, the auditorium stilled, not a cough, not a rustle of a sweet paper to tell of the presence of an audience.

He held his rapier straight out, aiming it the heart of the Roundhead Captain of Horse, as if telling him how he would meet his death. Kevin did the same, both men looking at each other over their swords without expression and without speaking. While below, the spectators, meeting at least that part of Rory's imaginings, had fallen silent.

'You owe me a death, Captain,' Rory said calmly. 'That of my son. And I am here, sir, to collect it.'

The two blades met, like boxers touching gloves, and were then lifted briefly in salute.

Rory stepped back and swiped viciously at the air a couple of times with his rapier, as if working off a little of the grief and anger his face was set with.

He took an abrupt step forward a few times, as if about to attack, before doing so, suddenly, as if out of that anger and grief, the rush met adroitly by Kevin on his blade, and a brief furious engagement followed, the swift dance of their steel throwing off shards of reflected light.

They circled each other, knees bent, left hands held out for balance, trying to read the other's next move, getting the timing right to strike, moving as if trying to get under each other's guard. Feinting, attacking and counter-attacking, parry and riposte, advancing and retreating, the dance of duellists.

They engaged again and again, in rapid, graceful bursts of speed and changes of direction, both quick and light on their feet. The hammered, workmanlike blows, steel on steel, ringing out, their breathing increasingly laboured in the brief pauses, rapiers held straight out again, watching each other intently over them, the shine of sweat on their brows.

Then Rory feinted for a last time, feinted right and in the same movement dropped into a lunge crouch, reaching with his front foot and pushing his body forward with the back leg, and thrusting upwards, to the left, a move practised over and over by the two men in rehearsal.

The buttoned point of the rapier passed between Kevin's body and the arm on the side away from the audience, as if through his heart.

The Captain bent over as if in pain, hugging the rapier to him, before sinking to his knees, and toppling to one side with a look of resignation, taking the sword with him. The look was not that of a man resigned to death, but having to again succumb to someone he considered to be an inferior fencer.

He'd made his feelings about that known, in small oblique ways. And had refused outright during the dress rehearsal, when in the uniform that was a declaration of who he was, what he stood for, his refuge from a world turned on by the Swinging Sixties, to accept Rory's filmactorish fencing flourishes. To indulge the flippancy of a booted gentleman-at-arms, the refusal to take much seriously, apart from drinking and the pursuit of women, of a Cavalier.

The last incident had involved Rory shooting up his left hand, and when Kevin, thrown off guard, had glanced up at it, tapping him on his lobster-pot helmet with his sword, as if it were some sort of game.

And fuelled by the sort of anger that had started a revolution, Kevin had attacked furiously, without the calculated precision of county-level fencing, and had had his sword knocked from his hand for his pains. And when he'd bent to pick it up, his offended dignity putting the blame squarely where he considered it belonged, the Irishman had struck him lightly, dismissively, on his rump with his blade.

He had threatened to leave there and then, and was only stopped from doing so by Phineas getting Rory to apologise, which he did – in an off-hand sort of way, suggesting that he didn't in the least mean it, followed by what to Kevin's scandalised eye looked very much like a seductive wink, confirming him in his opinion of actors.

Rory retrieved his rapier from under the Captain's arm, wiped imaginary blood off on the simple rough cloth of his Puritan faith, sheathed it and nodded once at the recumbent Roundhead, saluting the death of a fellow soldier. Then joined the remaining Cavaliers and the three women as if offstage in the corridor.

Which was Sion's cue to turn off the landing light, leaving the Dance of the Fallen lit only from the light in the hall.

Just before that he had added dry ice from the containers he'd kept in the bath, the block broken up earlier with a hammer, and smoke now dribbled from the nozzle, as if something very small had a cigarette on inside.

He switched on the machine and started slowly to crank out more smoke, more than he thought should come out. But it was his first time working it and it seemed to do what it was supposed to do, lying low, covering the fallen.

He thought it looked rather good, the figures of the swordsmen, led by Artemus, rising from the smoke, rising to fight again, their blades cutting soundlessly at the air in a rehearsed sort of slow motion, a ghostly echo of a long-ago battle.

From his position below the half-landing, standing on the stairs as if waiting to get past, Phineas took up his narrative again.

'The Dance of the Fallen. The spirit of young Artemus, and the soldiers of two sides of a riven country, carrying their differences into the hereafter. There are no ghosts, as far as is known, under this roof,' he went on, glad Jasmine had gone home. 'And unlike a certain establishment not too far from here, whose reputation I will not tarnish further by naming, we refuse to fix it, as the expression has it. To rig the pretence of such and to fraudulently charge money for it. But it is not too fanciful, surely, in this house that has seen centuries of history, to imagine that part of its past rising again, as it did this evening. We apologise for the rather cramped conditions from which you had to view it, but you can see our difficulties, striving as we did for historical authenticity. And if, despite that, you have enjoyed the evening, please do tell others. Our hosts,

Sir Humphrey and Lady Clementine Strange, need all the financial assistance they can get to maintain Batch Hall, part of the history, our history, you have seen this evening. Thank you.'

Sion had let the smoke fade during the narration, the fallen joining the upright out of sight in the corridor. And now, led by Artemus, leading this time the living as well as the dead, they all returned to the landing as if for a curtain call, and took the applause of their audience.

The mood in the Hall's kitchen, after the Sunday show was over and the re-enactors had driven back to Birmingham, was not buoyant. People had not so far, as Phineas had predicted they would be, been queuing up, despite fliers to local pubs and an ad in the *Kingham News*.

Saturday evening had seen eight paying customers. That evening the number had been reduced to six.

No one had turned up to pay at the door, as they had told themselves would be the case, then might be the case, telling it to themselves right up until it was obviously not going to be the case.

'Word will get around, you'll see,' Phineas said, as if speaking from experience.

'Word of mouth,' Rory added. 'It's how a lot of seats get sold in theatres and cinemas.'

'Yes, we've gotta give it time,' Shelly agreed, as she'd agree with almost anything Rory said.

'That word of mouth,' Sion said, 'might include getting a crick in your neck because you have to stand looking up the show from the hall or the stairs. Should have held it in the castle, as I said.'

'It didn't happen in the castle,' Phineas said. 'History had something else to say there. It's why Cuthbert Stanley and his merry men come back each summer.'

'And what if it rains, Sion?' Clem said.

'Yeah, well, all right,' Sion said, and helped himself to another Shropshire Dunk.

'And anyway, Sion,' his mother said, glaring indignantly at him, 'they get a free coffee and a hotdog – with Shelly's Stars and Stripes Extra-Special Relish on it. What more do they want for their three quid!'

Sion, busy chewing on his chocolate biscuit, merely shrugged.

'Perhaps it's the wrong time of year,' Rupert suggested. 'You know, coming up to Christmas, people saving their money.'

'Then I propose that we just sail on as we are,' Phineas said. 'Bows into the storm, as the Commander would advise, and keep the wardroom open.'

'Quite right, Phineas,' Clem agreed. 'And talking about Christmas, we'll get the tree in and put the decorations up next week.'

She seemed, as she had over the weekend, almost blithely unconcerned about the show's takings, putting a cheerful face on things, even for Clem.

Humphrey was out, driving Nigel to Shrewsbury to get a lift back with his work colleague. But had he been there, it might have occurred to him that his wife was a woman with something up her sleeve.

Chapter Thirty-One

The following day, Rory came back from the shop with his usual copy of *The Times* and a packet of Rothman cigarettes to go with his morning coffee, and found he'd had a phone call from his agent.

He phoned her back and came into the kitchen with the news that a film part he'd auditioned for, a couple of weeks before Batch Magna, had been successful. It wasn't a big part, he told them, and, as it was set in the 1940s, it required him to get his hair cut, but it paid well and would add to his film credits. And it would of course mean that they would have to enlist another Richard Strange from the rank of the re-enactors.

'I'm going home for Christmas,' he said. 'And rehearsals will start in the new year, so…'

'Rory,' Clem said, 'we will no doubt be able to get someone from among the club fencers with your competence, or near enough it. But never, never with your flair.'

'Humph, if you ever get round to selling this woman of yours,' Rory said, 'promise me you'll give me first refusal.'

'Well, I wasn't planning on doing it, but yeah, sure.'

'And don't you dare forget where we live!' Shelly said, indignant at the thought.

'He'd better not,' Annie added.

'Batch Magna,' Rory said, 'once met is surely never forgotten. I'll be back, and glad to. I'll nip over before I settle down with the paper and a coffee and tell Phineas. He's the one I owe for the great good fortune of having you people in my life.'

'Oh, the blarney,' Clem said.

'If I were thirty years younger,' Shelly said wistfully at the doorway he'd just departed through.

After Clem had left for a dental appointment, Humphrey followed with the shopping list he'd been given for the discount shop in Penycwn.

He put their three dogs in the back of Henrietta, their ancient brake, a wedding present from Clem's parents. Large and wooden framed, carrying dogs in the rear behind the six seats went back to before the war, dogs, along with loaders, guns, lunch hampers, game, back to a time when Clem's parents still had an estate. Her size, and pace, lumbering along the narrow lanes, suited Humphrey perfectly. He left belting along them, with double blasts of the horn on the tight corners to Clem in her fire-engine-red Mini.

In Penycwn he found a parking space in the high street under the Christmas lights. Further down the street the Salvation Army were playing, their voices ragged in a wind that had got up, but marching dauntlessly on into it.

Turning up the collar of his late father's Eagle Squadron flying jacket, he walked up to the discount shop.

His shopping list included more rolls for the hotdogs for the coming weekend, dressed with Shelly's relish using a recipe she'd brought across the Atlantic with her, an elixir which turned, as Phineas had put it, the humble Frankfurter into ambrosia.

He saw that Penycwn Castle, on a hill at the end of the high street, was flying the red dragon of Wales, the first time he'd seen it fly any sort of flag. The castle had been built by Norman hands, and had known the flags and tongues of both Wales and England over the centuries, as regularly as if they'd taken turns at occupying it. Owain Glyndwr, Prince of the Welsh Marches, in the end, the flag said, had had the last word.

Humphrey was quite taken by it, the red and green streaming out in the wind from the battlements, as if flying into battle, and decided to have one for Batch Castle. Have three flags in fact: the red dragon, the Cross of St George, and the Stars and Stripes.

When, that is, he reminded himself, they could afford to. When they had money to spare, he told himself, meaning more than that, looking away when he passed the window of a toy shop, guilt following him the rest of the way.

Chapter Thirty-Two

By the time he was walking through the doors of the Hall, Norman flags were flying from a Batch Castle bathed in the Technicolor light of a film he'd seen once. And Owain Glyndwr, who, Phineas Cook had said, Shakespeare had made a king, was wearing a burnished crown and sitting on a charger dressed in a cloth of his colours, his hand lifted to give the signal to follow him against the stone walls of the invader, when Annie came down the stairs with the vacuum cleaner.

'Oh, there was a phone call for you, Humph,' she said. 'An Arabella Beddoes. Would you ring her back, she said. Her number's on the pad there.' Annie indicated the telephone table in the hall.

'She sounds nice,' she went on, pausing on her way to the kitchen. 'Anybody I know?'

'No, she—'

'Sounded like that woman, I thought, the one who reads the news on telly.'

'I'd better ring her now, Annie. It might be important,' he said, cutting off whatever she was about to say next. Annie always had something to say next, and Clem could walk in at any moment.

Perhaps she might not be in, he told himself, ringing Arabella's number. Perhaps she'd phoned to say everything had had to be called off.

Arabella was in, and she hadn't called to say everything had been called off.

She told him that they were going to run the piece they'd put together after visiting the Castle when they next published on Wednesday.

'Wednesday of this week?' he said, seeing it closing in.

'Yes. But we won't of course mention your gift. The viewers will be told about that on the day itself. On Christmas Eve, when Father Christmas makes a special visit to a certain group of children.'

'Yeah. Yeah, and about that, Arabella,' he said, taking the plunge. 'See, the thing is—'

'Golly, it's rather like the real Father Christmas, isn't it, Sir Humph. If that is of course one believed still in Father Christmas. But if one did believe still, well, it would be just like it, wouldn't it. And just like the real Father Christmas, you will be delivering far more than toys. And to think this all happened in my first week, and on my first job. Which just happened to be a piece on the Christmas decorations at the hospital, when Matron mentioned you and your super gift. Christmas again. Makes one think, doesn't it.'

'Yes, yes, it does,' he agreed hurriedly, getting it out of the way. 'Arabella, I—'

'Oh, almost forgot. Bevers wants to—'

'Who?' Humphrey said, diverted.

'Bevers, Beverley Kynaston. Exec producer at ATV Midlands?'

'Oh, yeah, television.' He'd forgotten, had managed to forget, about television.

'Well, he wants to film you in your Father Christmas costume aboard the Castle next Monday, Christmas week, sitting in a mock-up sleigh the studio props department have put together – Bevers says it looks super! – to drum up interest in your ride into town. Not on a donkey,' she said with a little laugh. 'But on the back of a lorry which will be dressed like a Christmas float. They'll hire a crane for moving the sleigh, on the boat, and off it, and on and off the lorry. Gosh, this is fun!'

'Arabella…'

She waited. 'Yes, Sir Humph?'

'Arabella,' he started again, before deciding that if anyone should be told first of his foolishness it should be Clem, his wife. Not only putting off telling Arabella – someone else his lie, his gift at Christmas, had turned young again – but telling himself he was doing so for the right reason.

'Arabella, I have to tell you, you've done a swell job,' he said instead, and meant it, or something like it. He wanted to say something nice to her, and that was all he could think of. He thought her a very engaging, likable young woman, and he was sad that she in return would soon see him in a different light.

'Thank you, Sir Humph. But I believe – well, it's as if there's something, or someone, with far more power than I have behind it. It's truly like a Christmas miracle. Because you'll never guess! As well as regional stations, Bevers has had interest from national television, both the BBC and ITV. And even – drum roll – even where you come from.

Yes, you've guessed it. America! He's got contacts in all the major US stations. Your good deed, Sir Humph, will be seen from coast to coast. The power of that little candle flame. Even the winds of the Atlantic cannot put it out.'

She paused, and then her voice rose on a breathless, higher note. 'Sir Humph – Sir Humph, it's like the true meaning of Christmas. The birth on Christmas Day, and the hope it brings to all his children,' she said, and with a sort of choked goodbye, rang off, as if quite unable to say any more.

He stood for a few moments, phone in hand, staring at nothing. And then took off round the house, wandering up and downstairs, as if chasing the answer.

And when he heard Clem pull up in her Mini he decided to confess. He went outside to meet her.

A bit of a scrape and a polish, she told him, when he started by asking her how the dentist went.

'And you, my lad, have an appointment made for you for next Monday. And no excuses this time. I thought you Americans liked your teeth.'

'Yeah, that's right, we do,' he said absently.

'Well, there you are then. You can have them nice and shiny for Christmas.'

'Clem,' he said suddenly, with the force of confession. 'Clem, I've just been speaking to the woman on the phone, the one who did the magazine thing aboard the *Castle*, about Father Christmas arriving on it, and the children's ward in the hospital and all that. And—'

'What magazine thing?'

He looked at her. He'd forgotten that he hadn't told her, hadn't told her for good reason.

'Didn't I tell ya? I told somebody. Must have been Annie or Shelly. Yeah, that's right, you weren't here. You were at a WI meeting, or something – no, wait! I remember now, it was your mom and pop morning,' he said, meaning a visit to her parents forty-odd miles away in Shropshire, caretakers in their own house for the National Trust.

'Well, what magazine is it?'

'*Marches Life*. She wasn't sure if she could use it because of space. That's why I—'

'*Marches Life*…?'

'Yeah. I guess that's why I didn't bother telling you, because—'

'I've been trying for ages to get them interested in giving us some sort of mention. Even paid for an ad with them. That magazine goes right across the Marches. But their features editor simply wasn't interested.'

'Yeah, well this is a new features editor. But the thing is—'

'Look, shall we go inside. I'm dying for a cuppa.'

'Yeah, OK. Now, I—'

'So, they are running the piece after all, is that right?'

'Yeah, yeah, they're running the piece, but—'

'When? It's not long to Christmas.'

'Wednesday. It comes out Wednesday.'

Clem came to a halt. 'This Wednesday?'

'Yes, this Wednesday,' Humphrey said impatiently. 'But, honey, I have something I—'

'What's her name?'

'Who?'

'The features editor.'

'Her name? Her name's Arabella. Arabella Beddoes – why?'

'I want to give her a ring. Have you got her number?'

'Whaddya wanna ring her for?' he asked, as if her answer depended on whether or not he gave her the number.

'What, darling,' Clem said with exaggerated patience, 'happened last weekend? And what is happening again this coming weekend?'

'Yeah, yeah, I know, the ghost thing. Well what's that got to do with anything?' he said sulkily, his intention to confess retreating into where the old Humphrey lived still.

'Because, husband, if she's running a piece on you as Father Christmas she will, presumably, have to mention Batch Hall. And so might also be persuaded to also mention *The Artemus Strange Ghost Experience*. If only so that the players don't end up talking only to themselves. Might even cover it on the night. She might also feature, at some stage, the story, the true story, of Artemus Strange. It's called, darling, publicity.'

Humphrey opened his mouth to speak, closed it again,

'Yeah, all right. It's on the notepad on the telephone table,' he said, surrendering the details, surrendering to fate.

'Put the kettle on,' Clem said, nipping ahead, leaving him standing there.

'Yeah, all right,' he said.

After putting the kettle on for tea, Humphrey sat at the kitchen table listening to Clem on the phone in the hall, waiting for what he had coming to him.

The more they continued to talk the more likely that became. Annie had mentioned bringing in over the next couple of days the big Christmas tree they dressed for the hall each year, and which was kept in the orangery. Or rather what had been an orangery when the Royalists and Roundheads were murdering each other upstairs. The tree was in one of the large wooden tubs which in palmier days had held hibernating citrus trees.

Humphrey saw escape, or at least a stay, and got to his feet. 'I'm not doing anything at the moment, Annie. I'll get it in now,' he said, and sat down again, when Clem breezed into the kitchen.

'What a delightful young woman Arabella sounds. Very chatty. Quite unlike the previous editor. Who had a mouthful of plums and as much warmth as an ice lolly.' She smiled at Humphrey. 'She's going to mention the show in Wednesday's edition.'

'Great, honey,' Humphrey said.

'I thought she sounded nice,' Annie said.

'*And*, in the new year she's going to do a piece on Artemus. It screams local interest, she said. Very enthusiastic, she was.'

Humphrey nodded. 'That's Arabella.'

'Really taken with your offer to visit the children's ward as Father Christmas.'

'Yeah,' Humphrey said, and waited for the rest of it.

'And not only that,' Clem said, 'she's going to feature the *Castle* when the season starts. Take a ride on her with a photographer. And that magazine of theirs goes right the way across the Marches, B&Bs, hotels, pubs, as well as newsagents.'

Both Annie and Shelly thought that was great, and said so. Humphrey came in behind them, saying he thought it was great as well.

Clem sat down. 'Did you make the tea, love?' she said to him.

Humphrey looked at her, wondering if she meant something else by it, if she was teasing him about it. He had long learned that in this country there was English, and then there was English, a language that could still at times catch him out.

'Make the tea?'

'I'll do it,' Shelly said; making tea was the sort of English Shelly was fluent in.

'Was that all?' he said to Clem.

'Was that all what?' Clem said.

'Was that all she had to say, Arabella?'

'Yes. Why – were you expecting something else?'

'No, no – I just – er – you know, just wondered. I told you about the television thing, didn't I. So I wondered, if – er—'

'If anything had been changed? No, she didn't say anything,' Clem said, and smiled at him.

Humphrey stared at her, as if expecting a trap, and then said, 'Well, that's *great*, honey. Great. That's great,' he said again. 'I'll have that tea later, Ma,' he said to Shelly. 'I'm gonna get the Christmas tree in,' he added to Clem.

He left, glad to be on his own, frowning his way down to the orangery. He was wondering with vague suspicion what somebody was up to. That 'somebody', at times like this for Humphrey, could be almost anybody. All he knew at times like this, was that something was going on somewhere.

They were on the phone long enough, he told himself, and them, accusingly. So how come Arabella, who was always going on about his gift of toys, who seemed to see it as some sort of Christmas miracle, had not said a word about it to Clem?

It didn't make sense, it just didn't make sense, he told himself, wrestling the big tree out of the orangery, a grumpy Father Christmas, muttering to himself as he trudged up the yard, burdened with Christmas.

And it was because of Arabella and her enthusiasm for someone neither of them any longer believed in, that that promise, that lie, would now not only be made known, but would be in lights and serenaded with carols, with him, a Father Christmas with nothing in his sack, being borne in procession with sleigh bells ringing from Batch Magna to Kingham. And beyond, far beyond that little town, a promise that would then travel to television screens in sitting rooms across the country, and coast to coast in the homes of America. And beyond even that, to travel round the world, he wouldn't be at all surprised. Because of Arabella.

And it was because of Arabella that he'd been given, on this last weekend before Christmas, a chance, a last chance, to redeem his part of that promise.

A short while after that, with mugs of tea poured and the Shropshire Dunks out, the phone rang again.

By the time the first of the re-enactors had driven up the drive, Nigel, in his car with the wiring repaired, the rain blown across his headlights, seven more cancellations had been phoned in.

Nigel stood in the hall smiling at Christmas, at the decorations and the big tree, brought out each year since the family had moved in there. Its enduring green reaching beyond the height of the first-floor landing, the skirts of branches dressed with Christmas lights, baubles and tinsel, under a large guiding Star of Bethlehem. A home-made star, cut out by Humphrey on their first Christmas there from the bottom of a biscuit tin.

A couple of its points were creased now, where they had bent over the years and he'd had to straighten them, and the acrylic gold paint he'd used had worn thin in parts. But it was still bright, its story, cut from a biscuit tin, shining on with battered insistence.

By well before eight o'clock, all the other re-enactors had arrived. They had run into the worst of the weather when only within ten miles or so of Batch Valley, and sat in the kitchen with hotdogs and coffee talking about it.

By eight o'clock they had changed into their uniforms, and were ready, as the youngest member of them put it, to roll.

It was gone eight o'clock before they had anyone to roll to. Nine turned up altogether, and it became clear that they were all the audience they were going to get that evening.

'Are they British, or not!' Phineas ranted. 'Surrendering a night's entertainment to a drop of rain. And where's their damn manners, not to have phoned to tell us? And for God's sake, Lenny, get yourself a bit quicker up the apples tonight. Put a bit of *drama* into it, man, you're supposed to be galloping to the rescue,' he snapped, taking it out on a stooped gangling Cavalier, not naturally given to either speed or drama.

Phineas, starting his narration to his audience of nine, left out Humphrey hammering on the front door, because both sides were lurking in the kitchen, in the dry, waiting for their cue.

'The Parliamentary Captain of Horse with a few of his men, unaware that the main force of Roundheads had been defeated in their attempt on Batch Castle, smashed their way through the doors here, intent on plunder,' Phineas said, his words producing Kevin and his men from the kitchen, and setting the three women in the bedroom off, who, their door ajar on this occasion, had also picked up their cue from him.

'They hear female cries and charge up the stairs. Their cries have also alerted the son of the house, eighteen-year-old Artemus Strange, who with a lion's heart does not hesitate and lends his sword to their defence.'

Phineas took them through the death of Artemus and the meeting of Roundhead and Royalist steel, and the duel which ends with Richard Strange avenging his son, and then introduced the Dance of the Fallen.

'Young Artemus Strange was the first to fall and the first to rise again,' he told his audience, giving Nigel his cue, and watching the smoke roll along the landing, shrouding the bodies, their ghosts rising from it to do silent battle, the smoke drifting down the stairs almost as far as the half-landing.

'Rather more smoke on this occasion, Sion, than I thought was absolutely necessary,' Phineas said afterwards, during the usual post-mortem in the kitchen, after the audience and re-enactors had gone. 'If you don't mind my saying so.'

'I don't mind you saying so, Phin. Because it wasn't my fault. It's the machine. It's erratic.'

'Well, I'll have a look at it tomorrow,' Phineas said vaguely.

'I've had a look at it,' Sion said, as if that was the end of the matter.

'And…?' Phineas prompted, as if helping him out.

Sion shrugged. 'I couldn't see anything wrong with it.'

'Ah,' Phineas said, knowing that if Sion couldn't find anything wrong with it, then he, Phineas, certainly wouldn't be able to. Which no doubt meant that there was nothing at all wrong with it. Which in turn meant that it was Sion's fault, but that with his usual stubbornness he wasn't going to own up to it.

'Well, not to worry, Sion,' he told him, as if with a forgiving pat on the head, and turned to the rest of the table. 'And yes, all right, the numbers tonight are not a cause for celebration. But tomorrow,' he announced, 'is another day. *And*, may I remind you, one that is still fully booked. *And* I don't have to tell you that the weather here can change like that!' he said, snapping his fingers at it. 'Turn in our favour in minutes, and we've got twenty-four hours.'

'He's right. He's *right*,' Humphrey said, clutching at the straws offered, gazing into his friend's rallying grin, wanting to believe.

Chapter Thirty-Four

Before the re-enactors had left on Saturday evening, Rory, as he wouldn't be seeing them again, had invited them for a drink on Sunday, at six in the Steamer Inn.

'Six o'clock? They don't open till seven on a Sunday,' one of them pointed out.

'This is Batch Magna,' Rory was able to tell him. 'This part of the country makes its own weather, and Batch Magna, in the spirit of the place, makes its own licensing laws. Just use the side door when you arrive.'

'And park outside the church, just down from the pub, to not draw attention to it. The lights will be on in there, God being at home all day on a Sunday.'

God was indeed at home, the air alive with the sound of his bells, a quarter peal ringing out over the village for choral evensong, Humphrey adding his praise with the big tenor, as Rory and Phineas moved like burglars in the shadow of the pub to its side door.

Patrick at a cricket club meeting, Dilly his wife had opened up, dressed for it in a fuchsia silk dress and black pearls. A small scented middle-aged blonde under a large helmet of lacquered hair, trailing her two miniature poodles from one of the pub's two bars to the other, serving the few other customers who had taken advantage of the Sunday side door.

'Like a coach party,' she said with satisfaction, looking at the gathered re-enactors, who seemed to have arrived at the same time, brushing the rain off their topcoats and hair.

Rory told Dilly she looked good enough to eat, and wanted to know when she was going to let him take her away from all this. She waved away his blarney, and then, when he turned to get orders for the first round, touched at her hair.

When Kevin seemed to be at a loss what to drink, Phineas suggested he try what he called the wine of Batch Valley, Sheepsnout cider.

'What? Scrumpy!' Kevin said. 'I don't think so.'

'Scrumpy? *Scrumpy*!' Phineas said, as if unable to believe his ears. Then Dilly took over.

'Excuse me,' she said, in a voice which usually meant someone was about to be shown the door. 'We do *not*, mister, sell scrumpy here. This,' she went on, pointing with a magenta-tipped finger at the wooden barrel behind the bar, 'is real cider. From the wood. If you want scrumpy, go to one of the cider houses in town,' she added, pointing him in that direction. 'You'll find it on the bar counter in a nasty brown plastic barrel.'

Kevin looked embarrassed by the attention, and a little cowed. 'Well, I don't want scrumpy. That's—'

Phineas, feeling sorry for him, tried to set her straight, while knowing there was little point. 'No, Dilly, what he—'

'This is traditional cider, mister, this is. Made naturally, in this valley from our own apples. Sheepsnout, Sweet Coppin, Dabinett, Rustfair. Proper cider apples.'

Kevin tried again. 'Yes, well, I'm sorry if—'

'It's not pasteurised, it's not carbonated, and it's not tarted up with syrup, or laced with chemicals. Here, try it for yourself. Scrumpy, indeed. Whatever next!' she muttered, stooping to the barrel with a half-pint gl ass.

Kevin looked at her, and then at Phineas, who made a face at him, indicating that it was best to humour her.

'There you are,' Dilly said. 'Well, go on, take it. It's on the house.'

He took the glass and, lifting it, looked doubtfully at the contents, the cider moving in it like pale gold flames, the fire of apples with the heat of a late hot summer baked into them, and then took a sip. 'It's not bad' he said.

'Not bad!' Phineas echoed.

'No, I mean, it's – er—' Kevin looked at Dilly, and hastily took another drink.

'Actually,' he said, sounding surprised, 'actually, when you get over the – er – the sort of shock, it's rather quite good.' He sniffed at it, a member of a local wine club who never missed a tasting session. 'A clean nose.'

'So I should hope!' Dilly said.

Kevin drank again, swilled it round his mouth, and then swallowed. 'Good aftertaste, a good length finish,' he said judiciously. 'Good balance of flavours, apple and a sharp note of acidity. And something – something I can't quite put my finger on…'

Kevin drank again, and then again, in frowning pursuit of that elusive note.

Then he shook his head and looked amused, as if being teased and not minding terribly.

'Some tantalising little…' he said, before giving up with a chuckle, a rakish, throaty sort of sound, as if indulging its pert coyness.

And lifting his glass found it empty.

He took out a small black purse and opened it. 'My round, I think,' he said, a more expansive Kevin.

'Put that thing away,' Rory said. 'I'm still buying.'

A while later, sitting at one of the long tables with the others, Kevin, another pint of Sheepsnout in front of him, said he had to confess that he normally didn't go to pubs, but his in-laws were visiting and he couldn't stand his father-in-law.

'Can't *stand* the man!' he said, hitting the table in emphasis. 'He's a know-all, a bloody know-all. A bloody know-all who knows *bugger* all! And one of these days I'm going to bloody well tell him so!'

He looked round the table. 'It's my round. It's my round,' he said again, looking at Rory and poking his own chest.

Rory put his hands up. 'OK, OK.'

The talk at the table got round to the respective merits of the bands Led Zeppelin and Pink Floyd, with Phineas throwing in Creedence Clearwater Revival. Their hit, he said, 'Bad Moon Rising', was one of the greatest rock songs ever written, and to prove it started to sing it, out of tune but with enthusiasm, until Kevin banged the table again.

'Bloody awful.'

'Well, I didn't think it was all *that* bad!' Phineas said.

'No. It followed the tune,' Rory said. 'More or less.'

'Not just that one. All of it. All that stuff. Songs of the devil.'

'Songs of the devil?' one of the Cavaliers said. 'Blimey, Kev, what are you on?'

'He's right though,' Andy Littlejohn, sitting next to Kevin, said.

'You can laugh,' Kevin said. 'It was music spawned in the Sixties, along with free love, drugs and letting it all hang out. Violence, crime, have all increased since then. The moral code started to break down, things the Bible tells us are sins were legalised, women given more rights. The Sixties, my friends, was a cesspit.'

'We're only supposed to be playing at this,' Lenny the Cavalier said.

'He's not,' another Cavalier said. 'Want another Cromwell? Send for Kevin.'

'Nothing wrong with that!' Littlejohn snapped.

A Birmingham bricklayer's labourer, Littlejohn sought distinction in a life that was going nowhere, and had an eye on the rank of Roundhead sergeant. And Kevin was not only a captain, he was also pally with Cuthbert Stanley. Following Kevin's example he was also getting acquainted with Sheepsnout cider.

'Cromwell did a lot of good,' another Roundhead put in.

'But he was such a joyless blighter,' Phineas said, breaking off a conversation to do so. 'If it laughed, or you could drink it, and it wasn't water – ban it. He even banned Christmas.'

'And he closed the theatres. He was a ruthless, Bible-thumping, warty hair-shirt,' Rory said. 'If you say his name in certain parts of Ireland still today – duck.'

'He did a lot of good things for his country. And he took care of his soldiers. Promoted them from the ranks if he thought they were good enough,' Littlejohn said. 'And he was there fighting with them, in the thick of battle. I won't have a bad word said about him. Not in my company.'

Rory carelessly blew out smoke from his cigarette. 'You've just heard one. Several, in fact,' either Rory, or Richard Strange, said. Even Rory couldn't with certainty have said which.

'For God's sake behave, the pair of you. We've got a show to do,' Phineas said, the two men holding each other's stare across the table.

'Yes, let it stand, trooper,' Kevin said. 'There is work to be done,' he added, in more exalted tones than that of a captain, and with far loftier aims.

'We could do with another Cromwell today,' Littlejohn said, addressing it defiantly to Rory, and with Kevin in mind.

'So we could spike his head again on Westminster Bridge, and throw a party,' Rory said. 'Good idea.'

'Rory!' Phineas said warningly, and glanced at Kevin to keep Littlejohn in order.

But Kevin was listening only to himself. 'The purging hand of another revolution,' he said, as if gazing into its flames, his pale eyes bright with rebellion and several pints of Sheepsnout. 'The iron fist of another Cromwell on a country that's gone soft.'

'You volunteering, Kev?' one of the Cavaliers said.

Kevin came back to them. 'If called to serve,' he said simply, 'then yes.'

The Cavalier who'd said that if you want another Cromwell send for Kevin, laughed. 'There you are! I told you – our new Lord Protector.'

'And I'd be by your side, sir,' Littlejohn said.

'Of course you will, Andy, sucking up as usual,' a Cavalier called Liam said. He wasn't as tall as Littlejohn, but he also was a manual labourer, and it showed.

'You wanna watch that mouth of yours, Liam.'

'Or what?' Liam wanted to know.

Phineas stood. 'Gentlemen, gentlemen, please! You're supposed to have settled your differences three hundred bloody years ago. And anyway, drink up. It's time we were getting back. Though what sort of show you'll put on is questionable,' he said with a touch of asperity, making a virtue out of having been too busy talking to drink much.

Chapter Thirty-Five

They had a far bigger audience than anticipated, even though, when it was time for the show to start, it was still raining. They had the full booking of fourteen turning up, plus two couples on a night out together and, on Sunday, limited in choice.

It was, Shelly said, an omen if ever there was one, on this last Sunday before Christmas.

Phineas was so encouraged he gave a little welcoming speech, and handing round fliers said that he hoped that if they enjoyed the show they would spread the word.

It was, he said to Humphrey, the turning of the tide.

And when it came to the rescuing Cavaliers chasing up the stairs, even Lenny put a bit of speed and drama into it, that, and their shouts of 'Good old Charlie!' owing more to time in the pub than ideology.

The battle on the landing went well, as before, and left, as before, four Roundheads and a Cavalier joining Artemus as the fallen. The women slipped out then, past the bathroom where Sion was tinkering with the dry-ice machine, down the backstairs to the kitchen, to prepare the hotdogs and get the coffee ready for the end of the show.

It was the during the duel that things started to go wrong.

Kevin had appeared a little odd when leaving the kitchen with his men to charge the stairs, shouting, 'Make way for the Lord Protector!', even though Phineas had already cleared a path through the spectators. Leaving those who knew their Civil War history wondering why Oliver Cromwell hadn't followed.

There were further suggestions during the duel between the two men that something was not quite right. The usual calculation and precision of Kevin's swordplay was replaced increasingly with something very much like the sort of flourishes he had complained about Rory using, and he was given to odd shouts of seemingly pointless laughter.

And then the dry-ice machine started playing up. Instead of its usual dribble of smoke after Sion had poured in the ice, it was coming out as if he had started to crank it, which he hadn't.

Below, Phineas made a mental note to have another, more pointed, word with Sion.

When the rehearsed moves of the duel ended, and Rory went into the lunge position to finish it, Kevin wouldn't let him. Instead of allowing Rory's blade to slip between his arm and body, he blocked it, and carried the fight back to him, catching Rory off guard, and with another wild laugh driving him back.

'What the devil are you doing, man!' Rory said.

'Ridding the country of long-haired degenerate bastards like you!' Kevin yelled.

'As you can see, ladies and gentlemen, or rather hear,' Phineas said with a little laugh, 'we strove for historical authenticity in idiom as well as dress. The Civil War was not in the least civil,' he added, sharing it jovially with two young men in duffel coats and college scarves, doing a joint project on the period.

'Burn – burn – burn!' Kevin chanted above them, slashing away as if beating time with his sword, the ferocity of the attack sending Rory backing away from it so fast that he tripped over his feet and fell.

He scuttled away, using his heels to propel him. The rapiers had safety buttons on their tips, but could still do damage, could still dent a windpipe or skewer an eye.

'And so shall all his enemies fall! Die, libertine!' Kevin shouted triumphantly and, batting away the smoke he'd only just noticed, pulled back his arm to drive his blade home.

Rory, in a move perfected on film sets, rolled out of the way, and almost in the same movement jumped to his feet and attacked, cursing him in Irish, fuelled with the ancient warrior blood of Galway. And it was Kevin's turn to back, backing and slashing, shouting something about the despoilers of England's youth.

Rory feinted to the right, Kevin went to block it, and Rory brought his rapier round and up in one swift movement and dashed Kevin's sword from his hand.

Kevin bent to snatch it up, and Rory put a booted foot on his rear and pushed. He noticed the smoke then, when Kevin, sent sprawling, all but disappeared in it, and glanced towards the bathroom, where what he could see of Sion was kneeling over the machine and seemed to be shaking it, or hitting it.

And then Littlejohn ran at him, rushing with promotion in mind to avenge the indignity met by his captain. Rory defended easily, almost casually, but was then driven against the wall of the corridor by an enraged Kevin joining in again.

And Liam the Cavalier, who had watched the unrehearsed departure with interest from his prone position, seeing this, shot to his feet to help a fellow Royalist.

'Good old Charlie!' he yelled, invoking the name of their monarch.

Littlejohn responded immediately, turning to meet him, and yelling back, 'Stand up now, stand up now!', both men using words from songs of the period that were part of the Society's re-enactment events.

The fallen, rising in the smoke, and those still standing in the corridor, understood the words if nothing else that was happening. It was to them a call to arms, something they had responded to countless time during the re-enactment events.

'*But the gentry will come down and the poor will wear a crown – stand up now! Stand up now!*' the Roundheads sang in response.

'*In sixteen-hundred and forty-three those Roundheads they were after me. But I was on a winning spree, fighting for good old Charlie!*' the Cavaliers sang back, and the two sides engaged, the landing frantic with the sounds of battle in the rising smoke.

Phineas frowned up at it, and raised his voice. 'Authentic battle songs of the period,' he told the two students, who were standing now just a few steps down from the landing, busily taking notes.

'Where's all that smoke coming from?' one of the spectators asked, sounding worried.

'A small technical hitch, ladies and gentlemen. No need for concern, it's being attended to. The skirmish you are now seeing is—'

'Phineas, what the hell's going on!' Clem said into his ear, the two other women standing watching from the kitchen doorway.

'Who's in charge here?' a man demanded.

Phineas held him off with a raised hand. 'Clem, I haven't the remotest idea. I suppose I ought to sort of…' he said vaguely.

'I'll do it,' Clem said, grimly taking the stairs two at a time through the smoke.

'Can I have a word with whoever's in charge?'

The man wore a check wool scarf tucked neatly into a Gannex raincoat, and a porkpie hat, and was carrying a clipboard.

'Not now, my dear fellow, if you don't mind,' Phineas said, following Clem. 'We've got a bit of an emergency on. I'll be with you in a minute.'

'I'm afraid you'll have to see me now. My name is Simpkins, Councillor Simpkins. And I am attending in my official capacity.'

Phineas paused between steps.

On the landing Clem was having trouble breaking it up.

Then she yelped suddenly, half scream like a whistle and half shout, a sound that when she'd exercised the hunt's hounds brought all of them falling over each other to come to heel.

It had a similar effect on the combatants. They stopped, immediately, swords poised, as if stunned by the sound.

'Did you say Councillor Simpkins?' Phineas said,

turning and going with a smile back down the stairs.

'I did,' Councillor Simpkins said.

'Councillor for sports, recreation and entertainment, with special responsibility for health and safety?' Phineas asked, wanting to be absolutely clear about it.

'That's me,' he said.

And he would never be more so. He would never be more William Simpkins than he was now, as Councillor Simpkins. Councillor Simpkins was William Simpkins in full bloom, the flower from the bud. And he gazed with a sort of wonder at the breach of at least half a dozen health and safety regulations.

Humphrey, who'd had his dinner and then left for ringing practice, came home to find that they had lost another source of income.

That, as paying entertainment, they needed a licence for the show, and repeating just a few of Councillor Simpkins's remarks, it was abundantly clear that there was absolutely no point them applying for one. He also learned that Littlejohn the Roundhead, who was fortunately car sharing, had had to be ferried to casualty in Kingham General for a suspect fracture of the wrist, and two other Roundheads, including the Captain of Horse, Kevin Thompson-Miller, and a Cavalier, Liam, were in the first-floor bedrooms sleeping it off before driving home.

The good news was that Clem now not only knew where the gaming and drinks licences were, she also knew that they were in date, because Councillor Simpkins had insisted on inspecting them.

And Nigel had left a Christmas card for them.

Chapter Thirty-Six

On Monday morning a five-ton flatbed lorry, its load strapped down under a wrap, followed by a mobile crane, drove along Batch Magna High Street and down the side of the pub to the river.

Jasmine Roberts, with those of her brood not at school, came out to watch, joined by an assortment of villagers.

Father Christmas had arrived in Batch Magna, or at least his sleigh had, when the straps were undone and the wrap removed. Cherry-red-trimmed with white to resemble snow, its sides decorated with green and gold curlicues, and with gold-painted curved runners.

The runners were clamped to the deckboards of the pallet it sat on. The crane's four lifting chains were fitted to the pallet's side stringers, and a few minutes later the large sleigh and pallet were airborne. Lifted and slowly swung, swaying, towards the river, over the booking office and landing stage of the Cluny Steamboat Company, to the winter-bound PS *Batch Castle,* where Sion was ready to direct it to its mid-deck parking spot.

Humphrey, a glum figure in his Father Christmas outfit, was waiting with the Commander to do a short interview with Beverley Kynaston about the trip downriver on Christmas Eve from Water Lacy. He'd been told to his relief that he didn't need to bring his sack of toys with him today, just to sit in the sleigh and wave cheerily at the camera.

There was a time when his Christmas Eve had been as pleasant as anyone else's. Carol singing through the village in the late afternoon, sitting on straw bales under lanterns on a trailer pulled through the winter dusk by a tractor, hot toddies and mince pies in the pub, and the carol service from King's College on the radio. And then to bed, and an excitement that wasn't all that different from that of a much younger Humphrey at the thought of Christmas Day.

Now he was Father Christmas. And on Christmas Eve the PS *Batch Castle,* after steaming up to Water Lacy, the halfway stop on her summer daytrips, would be waiting to take him, a prisoner of his own foolishness, back downriver to a waiting Batch Magna.

Except of course that he couldn't allow that to happen. At some point in the week he had to confess. Had to face who he was, and how he would look then in the eyes of Clem and everyone else.

Beverley Kynaston had the enthusiasm of Arabella, telling him that he looked *marvellous,* my dear – that he *was* Father Christmas, being that sort of size, while a much smaller Humphrey inside smiled feebly.

Beverley, in a blue denim safari suit, Cuban heels, and a flowing silk scarf, was setting up what he called the shoot, with his camera man and sound recordist. The camera had the ATV Midlands logo on it, a station, Beverley had told him, with a *terrific* regional reach.

'But as we know,' he added coyly, 'it won't stop there, my dear, will it.'

Humphrey did know. And he sat in the sleigh with that knowledge after the interview feeling as if he were on view, as if publicly shamed in the stocks, trying for a cheerful grin behind his stick-on Father Christmas beard, and waving for the camera.

Chapter Thirty-Seven

Rory left the following day, after leaving presents under the tree. It surprised Clem for some reason to see that he had wrapped them himself. His present from them was a pair of pyjamas, because he seemed only to have one pair, with an odd top and bottoms.

Phineas had to confess that he hadn't got a present for Rory, and Rory made it worse by producing one for him, unwrapped, and in a bottle. They drank a glass each until the next time, before Phineas drove him to Church Myddle.

And later that morning Humphrey received another present, one which, as Arabella would have put it, made him want to believe all over again.

Mr Perkins, who, with his family, had stayed at the Hall while attending a local wedding, rang. It was his son Howard who had found Rupert asleep in the coach house, in an old car which Miss Wyndham had said was a Bentley Saloon.

Mr Perkins had mentioned this to a friend in Coventry who restored classic cars for a living, and his friend had shown an interest in looking at it with a view to buying it.

If, that is, they were interested in selling it.

'We are,' Clem said immediately, and when he said they could get over there today arranged a time.

'Well, twenty or thirty quid's not to be sniffed at,' she told Humphrey.

'Sure,' Humphrey agreed, wondering if that was enough for a sack of toys. 'And it's only rotting away out there. And we can put the camp bed in there for Rupe to sleep on next year.'

'If he leaves,' Clem said.

'Whaddya mean, if he leaves?'

Clem smiled, gave him one of her smiles, as he thought of it. 'We'll see.'

Mr Perkins's friend turned up with him after lunch. Clem had vaguely been expecting someone in a sheepskin coat and suede shoes. The friend Mr Perkins introduced as Wally Fisher was wearing an old army greatcoat over grease-stained overalls and workman's boots.

'It's a Bentley Weymann three-litre Saloon,' Wally said immediately when he saw the car. 'Nineteen twenty-six. This model won the 1927 Le Mans. Faster than a Bugatti, the motor that had the racing field to itself at the time. Big engine,' he said, looking at it. 'One of the first production jobs with four valves per cylinder. Bugatti himself called it the fastest lorry in the world. Needs a lot – a *lot* of work. Still, as it stands, I could give you three hundred.'

'Three hundred?' Clem said carefully, making sure she'd actually heard that amount.

'Three hundred…?' Humphrey echoed, seeing salvation.

Clem was about to grab at it, when Mr Perkins said,

'Wally, mate, as I said to you, these are good people, trying to keep a roof over their heads. Be fair. I've got a good idea of the market, asking around, and the figure I had in mind was a grand.'

'*What*!' Wally looked shocked. 'I can't do that, give the stuff away. I've got a partner to answer to.'

'Wally, see them as friends.'

Wally took another walk around the Bentley. 'Five. Five hundred. That's my last offer,' Wally said, producing a thick roll of banknotes with an elastic band round it from a side pocket of his greatcoat. He took off the elastic band, giving them a better view of all that money. 'Take it or leave it.'

Clem was about to take it, when Mr Perkins said, 'Split the difference. Seven fifty.'

'You'll bankrupt me, Stan. Yeah, all right, all right. Seven fifty. Yes?'

'Yes,' Clem said quickly.

'We'll pick it up with the low-loader after Christmas, if that's all right.'

He was assured that it was, and he started counting out the money on the car's bonnet.

'You've got time, I hope,' Clem said, 'for a cup of something before you leave? And I can give you a receipt.'

After they had left, Humphrey took Clem aside, saying he had something to tell her.

'Is it about the sack of toys?' she said, when they were out of earshot of the kitchen.

He stared at her. 'Yes,' he said then, finding his voice. 'How did you know…? Arabella, huh?'

273

Clem shook her head. 'The matron told me. She's a fellow member of the WI.'

'Oh.'

'Yes, oh.'

'Well, why didn't you say something! I mean, I—'

'I was waiting for you to. And I have to say that I consider the fact you didn't, that you felt unable to do so, doesn't say a lot for our marriage. You weren't the only one involved, you know. You brought me, as your wife, into it as well.'

He couldn't remember the last time he had seen her look so serious.

'Look – look, honey, I'm sorry it's not that. I – er… It's complicated, OK? It goes back a long way. I will – I promise – I will try to explain I will talk to you, try to tell you about it. But not right now. Please.'

Clem looked at him, as if undecided, then said simply, 'OK.'

He touched her face. 'Thank you. I'm glad you know. And this money means—'

'The toys?'

'Yes, the toys. Me and my big mouth.'

'It means we can finish the lodge in time for holiday lets next year, that's what it means.'

'Yeah, of course, of course.'

'I've already bought the toys.'

'Yeah, I – *what?*'

'From a little money still held in trust for me. It's the reason I went to see my parents. You weren't the only one with a secret.' She came near to a smile then, and walking away, said, 'A plumber, indeed!'

Humphrey looked blankly at her.

She smiled sweetly at him. 'On the phone that day. Your plumber.'

Chapter Thirty-Eight

The village hadn't seen that many people in it since Sir Cosmo Strange, Humphrey's great uncle, had brought the small flotilla of boats that would become the old Cluny Steamboat Company steaming into the home waters.

The shop stayed open and the pub took on two extra bar staff for the evening, both giving thanks to *Marches Life* and Beverley Kynaston's piece on ATV. It seemed that half the Marches, both sides of the border, judging by the accents, were there to see Father Christmas arriving on a paddle steamer.

The flatbed lorry and the crane were back, waiting for the PS *Batch Castle*. She had left for Water Lacy, helped upriver by Sion shovelling on the coal. She'd be met by Humphrey, driven there by Clem, a far more cheerful-looking Father Christmas, with a sackful of toys in the back of the shooting brake.

It was heard first, across the silence of the river, heard before it was seen by those down on the landing stage of the new Cluny Steamboat Company.

She threw her brightness before her into the darkness, her wash, churned by her side wheels, shining pale silver under it as she puffed her way round the last big meander, a sound system sending the song 'Sleigh Ride' out across the bare winter fields. She lit up the night, turned it into a carnival of coloured fairy lights, the boat streaming with them, Humphrey sitting mid deck in his sleigh under the incandescent light of theatre halogen lamps, courtesy of Neil the stage manager.

The Commander gave the steam whistle three blasts on the approach, and rang down for slow ahead to Tom Parr in the engine room, where Sion was resting on his shovel, seeing off the last of a gallon of cider.

When the *Castle* berthed, to more ringing of the telegraph, Sion came up to clip the crane's chains to the stringers of the pallet. Giving the thumbs up to the operator, he pushed the sleigh clear of the halogen lamps, and held it steady as it was slowly lifted, its ascent followed by Beverley Kynaston's camera man.

And then it was pulled straight up into the night, into the darkness, and when it was well clear of the roofs of the offices, catching their reflected light, the crowd that side fell quiet. He had appeared as silent as a dream, and in that surprised moment it wasn't Sir Humphrey of Batch Hall on the end of a crane's jib, but the Father Christmas they no longer believed in. Father Christmas riding the night in a red sleigh with snow on it.

And then it came down to earth, lowered into position on the back of the lorry. The lorry moved off, down along the river and back down the High Street, lit up like a float, its sound system merrily belting out 'Santa Claus

Is Coming to Town', Humphrey, his sack of toys next to him, waving from his sleigh.

There was a good turnout in Kingham, with carols and sleigh bells now on the lorry's sound system. The ATV camera man was wrapped up and wearing mittens on the open back of a Ford pick-up truck in front. While Beverley Kynaston and his sound recordist were travelling in a car behind, with Arabella and the magazine's photographer.

Through streets that would never to Humphrey seem quite the same again, acknowledging those who had stood in the cold waiting to see him, with a wave that when shown later on television Phineas would compare to that of the queen.

And then Father Christmas turned quite ordinary again, clambering down from the lorry with his sack at the hospital entrance, where the matron waited to welcome him and there were carol singers with lanterns.

He felt somewhat uncomfortable, entering the children's ward. He wondered how he should talk to them, before reminding himself that he talked to children every day, his own.

He gave the toys to the nurses by a Christmas tree, where most of their patients had gathered. Children who listened with awe to Father Christmas talking with an accent they had only heard before on television, or at the cinema. Feeling perhaps because of it that he really must be Father Christmas, that for them his mystery was somehow part of that distant and unreal world.

He then did a tour of the ward, visiting those who couldn't get up. Father Christmas giving them special attention, spending time by each bed, a Father Christmas who was near sometimes to tears.

Later that evening, in the bell tower of St Swithin's, Batch Magna's parish church, following a tradition older than his family in that place, Humphrey rang the largest bell of the peal, the tenor, four times before midnight. And then gave praise with it again, the full peal ringing out bell on bell in joyous celebration.

Chapter Thirty-Nine

Christmas morning with a better sort of sherry than was envisaged, Clem saw to that, to go with the mince pies in the hall, where a log fire burned and the presents were exchanged.

The kitchen smelt already of Christmas dinner. A goose roasting in the Rayburn cooker. A loin of pork in its tray with parsnips and chestnuts, waiting to go into the oven of the stove, and a ham ready for baking and glazing. And a Christmas pudding of course, mixed and steamed on Stir-up Sunday, when everyone in the kitchen took a turn at stirring it, from east to west, following the three wise men, and then made their wishes for the year ahead.

There were twelve seated at the polished mahogany table in the dining room, its leaves pulled out at both ends to extend it. Clem had redeemed the family silver she'd pawned in Shrewsbury, the table laid with it and the starched whiteness of Irish linen napery, and with crystal decanters and glasses.

Annie was with her family on the *Felicity H,* and Jasmine and her brood were spending the day with her parents in Bannog. But Phineas was there, and Priny and the Commander, and Miss Wyndham and Rupert.

Humphrey had driven over in the shooting brake to fetch the three estate pensioners from the Masters' Cottages, as he did every year, and Tom Parr had walked up from his home there, as he did every year.

There was talk and laughter at the table after he'd finished carving, and the company of good friends, with paper hats and the silliness of reading out mottos from crackers. And Christmas pudding and glasses of vintage port, among the toasts one to the General and to Bess, a Bentley Saloon left behind like a gift.

And when Humphrey returned from taking the pensioners home, he suggested a walk to work it off. There were no takers, for which he was glad.

He wanted to be alone with the contentment he felt. He wanted to put a distance between it, its source, and him, the better to appreciate it, and give thanks for it.

He walked through the village, exchanging Christmas greetings with his neighbours, across the bridge at the end of it built by monks, and up into the hills.

On one of the lanes up there, he stopped at a field gate to look down on Batch Magna, held in the palm of its valley. Looked down on the tower of St Swithin's, and the tall chimneys of Batch Hall seen through the stripped winter trees. As he had looked down on them on his first day there.

The day he had stormed the village like an invasion, an invasion of intent, plans for change. Come among the people there as an enemy of who they were.

Until who they were became who he was, who he really

was. Someone he'd had to travel three thousand miles to find.

He walked down through the tangle of lanes that had taken him round in circles that first day, as if playing with him. Down from the hills that sheltered his family, that had sheltered his family for centuries.

Back across the bridge over the River Cluny, a man going home.

Chapter Forty

Just over three months after that, when the first colours of spring cut into the earth like small healing wounds, Rupert, his job hedge laying finished, rose early one morning, tidied his room and left a letter on the dressing table for Clem and Humphrey.

He left a letter for Miss Wyndham as well, one that had taken much longer to write, dropping it through her letterbox before walking on.

Walking on into spring and the open road as the sun rose, taking in the world like a hibernating animal waking and finding it just as he had left it.

When Miss Wyndham came downstairs and saw the letter on the mat she knew what it said, if not how he had said it.

She read it in the kitchen after putting the kettle on, and cried then. Had a little cry, as her mother would have said, brushing it away with her fingers. Old tears, tears she hadn't shed for a long time.

Tears for both of them, for what might have been, and, a very long time ago, for what once had been.

Then she simply carried on, as her mother would also have said, did once say, all those years ago.

She fed the cats, did a bit of dusting, whether it needed it or not, and made a list of what she wanted from the shop. All the things she would do normally, gathering her life to her again, the life before Rupert. And if there was sadness in what she did, the way she did it, there was also a growing suggestion of something like relief.

Love met regularly at Batch Hall, usually, but not always at night. It had done so for over three hundred years. Its name was Artemus and Rhianwen, the maid Jasmine had seen on the backstairs, her face open to the sun of a first love like a flower.

That Artemus had been betrothed to the young governess in the schoolroom was a fiction of Phineas's. There was only one love for him, as there was for her.

It lived still in the room under the roof that had been hers, and where they used to meet. There and wherever else they could in the Hall, and in the summer fields, and the hayloft in the yard, where they had laughed and loved.

Rhianwen had married two years after he was struck down outside the schoolroom, but not for love. That belonged to Artemus. And when she died it went back there to him, to where they were young together, and had never left.

The End

Also available

When Sir Humphrey Strange, eighth Baronet and squire of Batch Magna, departs this world for the Upper House, what's left of his estate passes, through the ancient law of entailment, to distant relative Humph, an amiable, overweight short-order cook from the Bronx.

Sir Humphrey Franklin T. Strange, ninth Baronet and squire of Batch Magna, as Humph now most remarkably finds himself to be, is persuaded by his Uncle Frank, a small-time Wall Street broker, to make a killing by turning the sleepy backwater into a theme-park image of rural England, a playground for the world's rich.

But while the village pub and shop put out the Stars and Stripes in welcome, the tenants of the estate's dilapidated houseboats tear up their notices to quit, and led by pulp-crime writer Phineas Cook and the one-eyed Lt-Commander James Cunningham, they run up the Union Jack and prepare to engage.

The Batch Magna Chronicles, Volume One

OUT NOW

About the Author

Peter Maughan's early ambition to be a landscape painter ran into a lack of talent – or enough of it to paint to his satisfaction what he saw. He worked on building sites, in wholesale markets, on fairground rides and in a circus. And travelled the West Country, roaming with the freedom of youth, picking fruit, and whatever other work he could get, sleeping wherever he could, before moving on to wherever the next road took him. A journeying out of which came his non-fiction work *Under the Apple Boughs,* when he came to see that he had met on his wanderings the last of a village England. After travelling to Jersey in the Channel Islands to pick potatoes, he found work afterwards in a film studio in its capital, walk-ons and bit parts in the pilot films that were made there, and as a contributing script writer. He studied at the Actor's Workshop in London, and worked as an actor in the UK and Ireland (in the heyday of Ardmore Studios). He founded and ran a fringe theatre in Barnes, London, and living on a converted Thames sailing barge among a small colony of houseboats on the River Medway, wrote pilot film scripts as a freelance deep in the green shades of rural Kent. An idyllic, heedless time in that other world of the river, which later, when he had collected enough rejection letters learning his craft as a novelist, he transported to a river valley in the Welsh Marches, and turned into the Batch Magna novels.

Peter is married and lives currently in Wales. Visit his website at www.batchmagna.com.

Note from the Publisher

If you enjoyed this book, we are delighted to share also *The Famous Cricket Match*, a short story by Peter Maughan, featuring our hero Sir Humphrey of Batch Hall, defending the village with both cricket *and* baseball…

To get your **free copy of *The Famous Cricket Match***, as well as receive updates on further releases in the Batch Magna Chronicles series, sign up at http://farragobooks.com/batch-magna-signup

Printed in Great Britain
by Amazon